THE POLYNESIAN GIRL

A LESBIAN ROMANCE

VICTORIA RUSH

COPYRIGHT

Peering over the prow of our fifty-foot schooner at the rising sun on the horizon, I closed my eyes and breathed in the fresh scent of the ocean breeze. After a series of short but intense one-night stands, I was beginning to feel cheap and demoralized. Even though I'd taken the initiative in most of the flings, at the end of the day I'd always come home alone feeling shallow and empty.

The affairs had helped free me from the bonds of my passionless marriage and opened my eyes to the pleasures of lesbian love, but somehow I'd never been able to make any of the relationships stick. Even calling them relationships was laughable, given the longest ones never lasted beyond the occasional overnight stay. I needed to clear my mind and get away from all the distractions and temptations of the big city.

This chartered cruise was the perfect balm for my aching heart. With a tiny crew of three sailors and eleven passengers, I had plenty of time and space to collect my thoughts and recharge my batteries. In the absence of the usual big ship amenities, our private yacht provided a much-needed respite from the hectic bustle of the urban jungle. The only sound I could hear was the rhythmic flapping of the boat's sails in the gentle breeze and the peaceful slapping of the waves against the hull as our sloop pierced through the cobalt-blue water.

As the sole uncoupled passenger on our month-long tour of the South Pacific Islands, I was happy to curl up with a good book on the forward deck and feel the wind flowing through my hair. Although everybody went out of their way trying to keep me engaged, I made it clear I was content to be left to my own devices. I'd paid a hefty sum for this cozy cruise, and I just wanted to have some alone time to cleanse my soul.

"Another beautiful day in paradise?" the ship's captain Ben said as he leaned his arms on the rail beside me.

"Yes," I said, gazing off into the distance. "It's so quiet and peaceful I can actually hear myself think."

Ben pinched his eyebrows as he glanced over at me briefly.

"Is that what you've been doing up here? I thought most people came on these cruises to get away from all those distractions. You know, to free their minds and commune with nature and all that."

I turned my head and peered into Ben's weathered eyes. His dark skin was prematurely wrinkled, but his salt-and-pepper beard and chiseled jaw revealed a handsome, sea-worn face. I wasn't sure if he was making a veiled pass or if he was genuinely concerned for my emotional state of mind.

"Never fear, Captain. I'm feeling the weight of the world fall off my shoulders with each new nautical mile we pass through these azure waters."

"Happy to hear," he said, straightening his arms on the handrail. "Is there anything I can get for you? Are you hungry? I've got some fresh halibut or pineapple if you're in the mood for a snack."

"Thanks," I said, shaking my head. "I'm still feeling pretty full from that full-course breakfast your chef prepared for us this morning. But in another hour or two, some fresh fruit and seafood will be just what I'm looking for."

"I'll see what we can scare up. You're going to need a little extra energy for our planned excursion later today."

He pointed toward the horizon on the port side of the ship.

"We'll be dropping anchor in another hour or so at that small island. There'll be lots of hiking trails with plenty of local flora and fauna to explore."

I squinted my eyes in the direction he was pointing and saw a tall green patch rising over the blue expanse of ocean. Up to this point in our cruise, most of the islands we'd visited had been little more than shallow reefs and sandy atolls.

"Judging by its elevation above sea level, it doesn't look so tiny from here. Is this another uninhabited island?"

"Actually, this is the first inhabited island we'll be visiting on our tour. But we're unlikely to encounter any natives. There's a small tribe on the opposite side of the island, but they're not very accommodating to visitors. They like their privacy. In fact, they're among the most isolated people you'll find anywhere on earth. With hundreds of miles to the next nearest inhabited island, they've learned to become quite self-sufficient."

I stared at the island as it slowly grew larger the nearer our vessel passed. It looked dense and lush, with thin silver waterfalls cascading through the thick jungle foliage.

"As long as they don't feed on *foreigners* to mix up their diet," I laughed nervously. "Are you sure we'll be safe there?"

The captain chuckled as he wiped a wash of sea spray from the bow of the boat off his forehead.

"Not to worry, m'lady. The whole cannibal myth is overblown. There are very few tribes that still practice that custom anywhere in the world. These people are reasonably enlightened, considering their remote location. Missionaries passed through here centuries ago, instilling a modicum of Western values. Some of them even speak English. But we'll be putting in on an isolated section of the island. In the unlikely event we encounter any natives, they shouldn't give us any trouble. Just be sure to stay close together and not stray off the beaten path."

"I wouldn't dream of going off on my own, Captain. My jungle survival skills are nonexistent—cannibals or no. I'll be happy to join up with the group for this expedition."

As Ben returned to the rear of the ship to navigate us around the encroaching shoals, I watched the beautiful island as we sailed closer. The lush foliage and turquoise water surrounding the sandy beaches reminded me of the stories of my youth. I fantasized about being marooned on the isle like Robinson Crusoe, building a fanciful fort in the trees and catching live fish to feed myself. Of course, having a hunky partner like Mel Gibson or Brooke Shields to keep me company in my little blue lagoon would make it even dreamier.

Suddenly I felt a stirring in my loins that reminded me how long it had been since I'd felt the tender touch of a lover.

2

When we put in on the secluded beach and carried our provisions onto dry land, I marveled at the surrounding landscape. Unlike the other remote islands we'd visited so far, this one looked tall and imposing. A dense blanket of trees carpeted the steeply sloped mountains, rising to a flat crater hundreds of feet above sea level. I could hear the harsh trill of birds screeching from behind the blind as thick, shiny leaves rustled in the distance. A small reef encapsulated our lagoon in a little crescent, creating a shallow pool to wade through. It would be the perfect spot to cool off after lunch and a hike through the humid jungle.

I watched with fascination as the captain and his crew caught some fish in the lagoon then cleaned and prepared the catch on a wooden plank on the beach. I don't think I'd enjoyed a seafood meal so much in my entire life. Whether it was simply the succulent taste of the freshly caught snapper or the exquisite scenery, I savored every bite as I soaked up the spectacular view.

I'd brought with me a minimum of provisions—just

enough to fortify me for our planned excursions. Foam sandals for walking on the beach, hiking shoes for the trail hike, and a cloth handbag with a few bare essentials: a bikini for a swim in the lagoon, some sunscreen and lip balm to protect me against the sun, and my smartphone to read romance novels during quiet moments. After we all finished lunch, the captain stood up to address the group.

"I hope you all enjoyed our impromptu picnic lunch. We'll be spending the rest of the day on the island and setting anchor for the night. For those of you still finding your sea legs, a calm sleep in the lagoon under the stars should help quiet your stomach. In a few minutes, we're going to organize a little inland hike. If you prefer to stay on the beach and have a swim or collect shells, our first mate Mike will stay behind to keep watch on our belongings. The rest of you can join Will and me as we explore the amazing landscape of this island. There's some beautiful wildlife and waterfalls, and at the top of the island there's a dormant volcano from which you can see a spectacular view of the Pacific for miles around. Before we head out, does anyone have any questions?"

One of the young couples raised their hand.

"Yes, Tricia," Ben said, nodding at the couple.

"Do we need to bring any special protection with us? I mean, are there any dangerous animals like monkeys or bears? I heard there are some tribespeople on the island. What should we do if we encounter someone?"

Ben chuckled at the familiar question. It never failed to amuse him how ignorant city slickers were of local customs.

"The islands of the South Pacific are actually some of the safest places in the world in terms of wildlife. There are no mammals other than harmless fruit bats and the local tribespeople, who are far away on the other side of the island. The only creatures that might harm you are brown tree snakes and mosquitoes. Just keep your head away from overhanging branches and wear lots of insect repellant and you should be fine."

Ben and Will passed out some silver whistles connected to a key chain.

"In the unlikely event that we should encounter a native person in our travels, do not approach them unless they approach you. They generally like to keep to themselves and won't engage unless provoked. Keep us in sight at all times and don't stray too far off the path. If anybody should get separated from the group, just give us a tweet using these whistles so we can find you. If for whatever reason you get lost, just follow the trail down to the shore. We plan to be back to the boat around five p.m. local time."

After collecting our gear and fastening our whistles to our belt loops, we followed single-file behind Ben along a narrow trail into the woods, with Will taking up the rear. It didn't take long for the brush to thicken, and as I swatted the thick leaves aside, I kept glancing upward for any sign of slithering reptiles. The one thing I feared more than anything was snakes, and I could feel my heart beating in my chest as much from the fear of being bitten as from the exertion of the steep climb. I was glad when our path crossed the occasional stream, giving me a chance to soothe my hot and aching feet in the cool running water. After an hour or so, we passed another creek and I sat down on the bank to tighten a loose shoelace.

"Everything okay?" Will asked, pulling up behind me.

"Just a loose string," I said. "You go ahead, I'll catch up in a few seconds."

Will peered ahead, noticing our group turning a corner in the dense forest.

"Are you sure you'll just be a moment? We don't want to get too separated from the rest of the group."

"Yes, I'll be fine—I promise." I patted the whistle hanging from the belt loop on my cargo shorts. "Besides, I can always give you a ring if I can't find you, right?"

"Yes," he said. "But it's always best to maintain line-of-sight. The terrain up here is pretty steep and treacherous. We've had people fall and twist an ankle. Just be careful. I'll be walking slowly ahead."

As Will continued up the trail and turned around the corner out of sight, I paused to take in the peaceful sound of the forest. Besides the occasional call of a distant bird, the only sound I could hear was the soft gurgling of the water as it tumbled over the mossy rocks. After I finished tying my lace, I hesitated when I heard an unusual sound emanating from the forest a few hundred feet upstream. I turned my head and strained to listen, then my eyes widened in recognition.

It was the sound of a woman's voice. A sweet, lilting sound, like she was singing. I squinted through the dense thicket of trees, then my eyes grew wider as I recognized the familiar figure. She was standing under a waterfall, stark naked and rubbing her body like she was taking a shower. It was hard to tell how old she was from my distant location, but she had the slender, lithe figure of a young girl. I glanced up the path in the direction Will had headed then back toward the girl.

What the hell, I thought. *I'm on vacation. Everyone says the best way to enjoy a different culture is to go native. I can always catch up with the group later. If Will is really worried about me, he'll double back to find me. Worst-case scenario, I'll have to wait for them to return along the same path on their way down, or I return to our cove. But this is some local fauna definitely worth exploring.*

I followed the tributary upstream, picking my way carefully over the slippery rocks and boulders. As I got closer to the girl, her voice became louder and I found myself humming softly, mimicking her lilting tune. She was speaking a language I'd never heard before, but the melody was simple and rhythmic. I flashed back to another one of my favorite fairy tales from my youth, when the English explorer John Smith stumbled across Pocahontas by a waterfall in the forest. The closer I got to the girl, the more mesmerized I was by her. I could only catch fleeting glimpses of her through the breaks in the heavy brush, but it was quickly becoming apparent that she had the body of a goddess.

When I reached a clearing about fifty feet away from the waterfall, I stopped next to a tree and gently parted the branches blocking my vision. When I finally saw the girl close-up, I gasped. She couldn't have been much beyond her teens, but she was stunning. With thick, shiny black hair cascading over her shoulders and breasts, her pouty lips and high cheekbones reminded me of a young Halle Berry. Her body had all the same curves and swells of her Catwoman avatar, except in this case, she was completely naked.

As I watched the water splash over her full breasts and hourglass-shaped hips, I couldn't stop gawking at her like some kind of creepy peeping Tom. I didn't even know if she was of legal age, if that even mattered out here in the remote stretches of the Pacific Ocean. But when I saw her hand disappear under the triangle-shaped patch between her legs and she began moaning under the torrent of water, I couldn't help myself. It had been far too long since I'd had any kind of sexual contact, and here was the girl of my dreams putting on the sexiest live show I'd ever seen.

I thrust my hand down the front of my cargo shorts and began circling my slippery pearl, trying to stifle my own moans of pleasure. Within moments, I felt the rising swell of my passion beginning to overtake me and I rested my left arm on the tree trunk to support my quivering legs. Just as I was about to be overtaken by my climax, I felt a strange object slithering up my arm. As I turned my face in shock to see what was crawling on me, I stared directly into the eyes of a long brown tree snake.

I had just a moment to scream and flinch my arm away before the snake lunged forward and embedded its fangs deep into the flesh of my neck. Within seconds, I began to feel faint and numb as my legs suddenly collapsed beneath me. As I crumpled to the ground beside the tree, the last thing I remembered was the shocked look on the face of the pretty native girl as she watched me lose consciousness on the moss-covered ground.

3

———

I woke up on the hard floor of a stick-frame hut, peering through bleary eyes at the interwoven leaves covering its thatched roof. An old native woman sat cross-legged beside me, holding a smoky bowl under my nose. The aroma was pungent, and I instinctively flinched my head to the side. The pretty girl I'd seen at the waterfall kneeled by my other side, holding a wet compress against my neck. I felt dizzy and weak, and my head throbbed with pain. When I tried to speak, I realized that the left side of my face was numb.

"Wh—where am I?" I said in a slurred drawl, trying to lift myself up on my elbows.

The girl smiled at me as she removed her hand from the side of my neck. I noticed a green paste on her palm, which she wiped off with a heavy cloth next to a wooden bowl containing what appeared to be a long animal bone.

"You're in our village," she said in a strange accent I'd never heard before. "You're safe now, but you need to rest. You're still weak from the after-effects of the *gata* bite."

She placed her other hand on my chest and gently pressed me down on top of a scratchy mat.

"Gata?" I said, pinching my eyebrows in confusion. "How did I get here?"

"It's our native snake. Normally, it doesn't cause this much trouble, but it struck you in the neck and the poison traveled quickly to your head. I had to carry you back to our village."

"*Carry me?*" I said, wondering how her small frame could support my weight. "How far?"

"I guess it would be more accurate to say I dragged you. I built a rough stretcher out of tree branches and vines. It took almost a full day to bring you back to our village."

I paused as I looked at the girl quizzically.

"Where are my travel mates? I came with a dozen other people—"

"If you're referring to the people on the sailboat, they stopped by our bay a few hours before we arrived asking if anyone had seen a yellow-haired European woman. The chief wasn't very happy with their intrusion, and when he said he hadn't seen any other foreigners, they sailed away."

"Away?" I said, shaking my head in dismay that they would abandon me so quickly. "Does that mean I'm *alone* on this island?"

The girl reached out and clasped my hand in hers as she smiled at me warmly. A group of young naked children suddenly rushed into the hut giggling, and the old lady shooed them away.

"You're hardly alone here," she said, glancing up at the woman who was still holding the smoking cup under my chin. "My family and tribe will care for you until your friends return."

The old woman said something to the girl in their native

tongue and I flinched again, smelling the strong vapor rising from the bowl.

"What's this strange smoke you're having me inhale? It smells like incense—"

"It's burning hibiscus leaves. We've found that it helps neutralize the effects of the toxin. Since you were unconscious, it was the only way we could get the medicine inside you. But now that you're awake, there are some more potent herbs you can take internally."

The old woman reached down beside her and lifted a coconut shell filled with a milky substance and raised it to my lips. She smiled at me softly and nodded for me to drink the elixir.

"What is that?" I said, frowning from the pungent smell of the mixture. "It smells like something died in there."

The girl chuckled as she squeezed my hand.

"It's made from the same natural ingredients that I've been using to neutralize the pain and swelling on the side of your neck. It's a mixture of plantain leaves, papaya bark, and turmeric, dissolved in coconut milk. You have to trust us. We've been administering this medicine for hundreds of years, and we know it works. I think you'll find the taste quite pleasant."

I reluctantly lifted my head and parted my lips as the old lady tilted the bowl toward my mouth. The potion was thick and grainy, like a soup broth, but it tasted more like chocolate milk. I swished it around in my mouth for a few seconds, then gulped it down nervously. The old lady looked into my eyes and nodded as she tilted the cup higher.

"*Sila atu,*" she said in a heavy accent.

"Drink the rest," the native girl said. "It will help settle your stomach and ease the pain."

I slowly emptied the bowl, then the old lady got up and said something to the girl before she stepped out of the hut.

For the first time since I'd woken up, I began to feel a little less anxious about my situation, and I gazed up at the native girl, studying her face. She was even more breathtaking close-up than I'd remembered. Her large brown doe eyes, small slender nose, and spongy cheeks gave her the appearance of a girl far younger than her sexy figure would suggest. I glanced at her chest and was disappointed to see that she was fully covered with some kind of dyed dress. The cloth looked thick and dense, more like a mat than the woven cloth used to make our Western garments. I glanced down my own body and was relieved to see that I was still wearing the same clothes I'd left the boat with.

"How long have you and your family lived here?" I asked, interested as much to learn about the history of her culture as her actual age.

"Our family and those of our tribe have lived on this island for centuries. As best we can tell from the oral traditions passed down from our ancestors, the island was settled by Polynesians traveling from the larger islands around 300 AD. I myself have lived in this little hamlet my entire life, which I'm told is eighteen rainy seasons."

So young, I sighed. With her flawless brown skin and soft cheeks, she looked even younger than her chronological age. I flashed back and remembered what she looked like naked under the waterfall, and shifted uncomfortably on the mat beneath me. I could feel the wetness building between my legs and blushed suddenly, realizing how attracted I was to this island goddess.

"You look even younger than that," I said, glancing at her tight-fitting frock. "At least, from the neck up. You're very pretty."

The girl smiled at me as she leaned in closer and lowered her voice.

"I saw you watching me," she said. "And I saw what you were doing behind that tree."

"Um..." I stumbled, not knowing how to react at being found out.

"It's okay," she said. "We're very open about our sexuality in our tribe. It's perfectly healthy and normal. I'm glad that you saw me. I think you're very beautiful also."

I felt a sudden tingle between my legs as I squeezed my thighs together, unconsciously rubbing myself against my tight cargo shorts.

"Oh?" I said, fishing for more details. "Have you had a lot of experience in that area? Where I come from, girls don't usually become active until your age or later."

"Most of the boys and girls in our tribe become sexually active soon after they reach maturity. But since I'm the daughter of the chief, he expects me to save myself until marriage."

"Now I see why you needed to find another form of release under the waterfall."

The girl smiled at me as I began to feel the perspiration building between our palms.

"A woman can only go so long with unsatisfied needs—"

"I know the feeling all too well," I nodded. "It's been a long time for me too."

The girl's eyes widened in surprise as she rubbed my ring finger with her fingers.

"You're not married? I would have thought a pretty woman of your age would have plenty of suitors..."

"I was, once. But my interests seem to have gravitated more toward women these last few years..."

The girl shifted her weight off her knees and sat cross-legged beside me, pulling the heel of her foot under her dress against her crotch.

"So have mine lately."

I paused for a moment, wondering how far I should take our little flirtation.

"You've never even been *kissed*?" I said.

The girl chuckled as she looked towards the front door of her hut.

"Not unless you count all the pecks on my cheek by my *matua*. I'm expected to remain chaste until the day I'm given away."

"Given away?" I said, shaking my head in confusion.

"Any potential mate must first be approved by my father. Not many suitors have stepped forward in deference to his authority."

"How many men are there in your tribe of marrying age?" I asked. "I can't imagine *any* young man or woman not being attracted to your physical beauty."

"It would have to be a man," the girl frowned. "It's considered *tapu* for a woman to sleep with another woman after she's reached childbearing age.

"That's a shame, because it's a singular pleasure to be properly kissed by a girl."

She paused for a moment as she looked longingly into my eyes.

"I suppose it wouldn't be a sin if we were to kiss briefly. My grandmother says the exchange of saliva acts as a potion in the case of snakebite. Something about the built-in immunity I've acquired from so many of my own snake bites. In this case, it would be more medicinal—"

I pulled the girl's hand toward me as I lifted my head up to her face.

"What's your name?" I whispered in her ear.

"Teuila. It means red flower in our native language."

"My name's Jade. It means pretty green stone in my language. Kiss me, Teuila."

The girl leaned forward, and when our lips touched, it was like a lightning bolt passed through me. I could feel goose bumps on my arms as my heart pounded in my chest. As she pursed her lips awkwardly against mine, I felt the sweet taste of her wetness filling my mouth. But as I reached up with my hands to cradle her head, I heard the loud flap of the blanket covering the front door sweep aside and the thud of heavy footsteps on the wood lattice floor.

"*O le a lea?*" a gruff middle-aged man shouted in front of the doorway, flanked by the older woman who'd treated me earlier.

Teuila shot up into an erect position and said something in her native language to the man. He looked at me with an angry expression and continued talking to her in an agitated manner. It was apparent from her submissive body language that the man was her father and the chief of the village. He obviously disapproved of a foreigner in his house as he pointed at me and motioned with his finger in the direction of the beach. He continued berating Teuila for many minutes before storming out of the hut and down the front steps. The older woman said some gentle words, then followed the man out of the hut as I heard them talking some distance away.

"I'm guessing that was your father?" I said.

"Yes," the girl said. "I suppose it was a bit of a surprise to find a strange European woman lying in his house after he'd been out fishing all day."

"He seemed a little angry," I said. "Was it because of our kiss?"

"I explained to him that I was trying to administer *pulu*,

but I don't think he was very convinced."

"What was all that gesturing about when he pointed at me and then toward the sea?"

Teuila exhaled heavily as her lips tightened into a frown.

"He said that he wants you off the island as soon as possible. If your friends don't return soon, there's a cargo ship that passes by here every month or so, where we exchange goods. He insists on your being on that ship by the latest."

I glanced up at Teuila, grunting as I tried to sit up.

"In the meantime, where do you want me to stay?"

"You're still weak and sore," she said, easing me back down onto the mat. "You're welcome to stay with us until you're fully recovered. I'm sorry to have put you through all this. My father can be a little hard-headed sometimes. I'm sure he'll come around once we explain the situation. How are you feeling?"

I smiled at the native girl and reached back out for her hand.

"I was feeling much better when you were administering your magic elixir. If the coast is clear, can I have another one of your healing kisses?"

Teuila turned her head as she watched her father and grandmother walking slowly toward the other end of the village.

"Maybe for just a few more minutes..."

She leaned down to kiss me, and I reached up and ran my fingers through her soft hair. When our lips touched, I gently probed her mouth and played with her tongue, tasting her sweet salve. Teuila moaned softly, as she rolled her hips over her splayed skirt on the floor.

This won't be the only waterfall we'll soon be experiencing, I thought, feeling my panties begin to rapidly moisten.

4

——————

Later that day, the chief returned to the hut, and he and Teuila had a calmer discussion. His countenance seemed to have changed completely toward both of us, and he nodded as he made eye contact with me before leaving to attend to other business. Not long after, the old lady entered the cabin carrying a platter of food and some fresh water. She spoke with Teuila briefly, then she kneeled down beside me and felt my forehead, encouraging me to drink the cool water. I was beginning to feel stronger, and I was able to sit up as the two women tended to me.

"Your father seems less angry," I said. "Should I thank your grandmother for that?"

"Probably," Teuila nodded. "When she explained the circumstances of your arrival and reminded him of our longstanding tradition of giving refuge to wayward travelers, he softened up. In fact, he insisted on holding a ceremony this evening to celebrate the rapid recovery of our honored guest. Do you think you'll feel well enough to attend the festivities?"

"Will it require my active participation?" I said, still feeling a bit sore and lightheaded.

"Not unless you want to. It mostly involves a lot of singing and dancing. My father has asked that we prepare a special feast for the occasion. There will be lots of local dishes for you to sample. All you really have to do is watch and eat. You haven't had anything in over twenty-four hours. It will be good for you to regain your strength."

I looked at the large platter of food that the old woman had placed on the floor beside me and smiled at her.

"I'm beginning to feel my appetite coming back. Is this all for me?"

"*Ai meaai,*" the woman nodded, holding the platter up and motioning with her hand toward her mouth.

The tray was filled with pieces of sliced banana, papaya, fresh fish, and some kind of shaved gourd. In the corner of the board sat a hollowed out half-coconut shell filled with the same creamy brown fluid the woman had administered to me earlier.

I looked at the plate, inhaling the rich fragrance of aromas, then peered up at Teuila.

"Is it okay to eat it with my hands?" I asked, not seeing any utensils.

"Of course," she said. "That's the only proper way to enjoy good food. Dig in!"

I picked up a slice of papaya, and when I bit into it, I closed my eyes, humming in appreciation.

"Oh my God," I said. "That is *so* good. It's so much more flavorful than the fruit I buy at my local grocery store. Do you grow all of your food on the island?"

"Absolutely. We have a great variety of fruit, vegetables, and seafood. The gods have blessed us with an abundance of natural resources to allow us to be self-sufficient."

I picked up a piece of white fish and sucked it slowly into my mouth. It appeared to be raw and marinated in some kind of citrus seasoning. Unlike the fresh snapper our charter chef had cooked up on the beach yesterday, this seafood was far more tender and juicy.

"You're spoiling me," I said, purring as I savored the succulent flesh. "This is the most tender seafood I've ever tasted. What kind of fish is it? And what's the seasoning? It tastes so simple and pure."

"We call it *fa'aipoipo*, but I think you call it halibut. It was fresh-caught today by my father and his fishing crew. We've added nothing but fresh lime juice to season it."

I shook my head at the simplicity of the native diet. I'd always felt that the best food needed little extra embellishment if it was truly fresh. And you couldn't get much fresher than this—from sea to plate in a matter of hours.

I took a sip of the coconut milk, then picked up the large pear-shaped tuber and took a small bite off the tip. It tasted a bit like sweet potato, but I also detected traces of the fresh seafood and papaya juices that covered the wooden board.

"What's this interesting fruit? It's got a delicious texture and flavor. I've never seen it before."

"It's one of our staples," Teuila said. "The taro root is actually a vegetable, not a fruit. We use it in much the same way that Westerners use potatoes. It's a very nutritious side dish that soaks up the flavors of other foods it's paired with. Do you like it?"

Holding the curved tubular vegetable in my hand, it reminded me of one of my favorite sex toys that I'd use on lonely nights to stimulate my G-spot.

"Mmm," I said, sucking the rich seafood juice from the tip of the bulb while raising a suggestive eyebrow at Teuila. "I'll definitely have to try more of this. I can imagine *all sorts* of ways it can be paired with other delectable dishes."

After I devoured the rest of the food on the serving plate, the old lady smiled at me and said something to Teuila.

"We should probably start getting you ready for the celebration tonight," she said, glancing at my soiled hiking clothes. "You must be looking forward to a bath. Let's get you cleaned up and into some fresh clothes. There's a private section of the lagoon where I can take you if you're strong enough to walk. Then my matua and I will prepare you with our local costume for the festival."

My pussy suddenly pulsed at the thought of bathing privately with Teuila.

"You're really having me go native, aren't you?" I said. "I think a swim in the lagoon would be very refreshing. I shouldn't have any trouble walking as long as you stay close by my side."

"I wouldn't think of leaving you," Teuila smiled. "Besides, I saw the way some of our young tribesmen looked at you when you came into our village. I need to make sure they don't get any ideas about the sexy white girl in their midst."

5

As Teuila escorted me toward the bathing lagoon, women and children smiled at me from the open verandas of their huts flanking the main thoroughfare of the village. But a group of men carving a dugout canoe on the main beach eyed me suspiciously when we veered off onto a flagstone-lined path leading into the woods. When we reached the secluded lagoon, I peered around me at the natural splendor of the landscape.

"Your island is so beautiful," I said, inhaling the fresh onshore sea breeze. "Where I come from, people pay a small fortune to visit these tropical paradises. And here I am, being feted by my native hosts, with never a thought to any kind of compensation."

"At least for a few more weeks," Teuila frowned, reminding me of the cargo ship pickup that was scheduled to pick me up later this month.

"If not earlier, if my shipmates return before then." I glanced toward the thick canopy of trees lining the lagoon. "If I hide in the forest, will you tell them I'm still lost? I'm in no hurry to leave this Shangri-La."

"I'd be happy to, but I think my father will have other ideas. We have to be careful not to test his patience too much. He's very suspicious of European visitors overstaying their welcome. He's heard stories of the destruction they brought to some of the other Polynesian islands."

I nodded, recalling how the indigenous people of Easter Island were nearly wiped out by disease and infighting after Dutch settlers arrived.

"I can appreciate why he'd want your people to be left alone. But you'll have to stop referring to me as *European*. I'm actually from the United States. I'm technically an American."

Teuila chuckled as she shook her head.

"They're just another colonial oppressor as far as he's concerned. He doesn't trust anybody who travels to these islands on fancy boats and planes. He thinks you'll corrupt our simple and natural way of life."

"He's probably right," I said. "Lord knows, our so-called advanced civilization has plenty of shortcomings."

I looked at Teuila's simple one-piece toga and motioned to my soiled clothing.

"Shall I take these off and leave them on the beach? Will you be offended if I swim in the nude?"

"Not at all," Teuila smiled. "It will give me a chance to clean your garments while you cool off. We all swim naked when we're bathing in the lagoon."

I glanced around me to see if anyone else was stealing glances from the surrounding brush and slowly began to disrobe. I knew that if anyone wanted to gawk at the white woman while she bathed that they could easily hide undetected behind the thick blanket of foliage, but I didn't really care. There was something about this remote island that seemed so natural and carefree to me. I was far more mindful of the impression I'd leave with the pretty native girl.

I turned my back toward Teuila, then pulled down my cargo shorts and panties, and slipped off my sweaty t-shirt and bra. It felt good to be liberated from the vestiges of Western civilization, and for the first time in my week-long tour of the South Pacific, I slipped into the warm waters of the tropical lagoon completely naked. It felt exquisite to be immersed in the buoyant salt water, and for the longest time I just floated on the surface, watching the wispy white clouds pass slowly over the sky. When I caught sight of the thin contrails of a jet aircraft high up in the atmosphere, I couldn't help smiling.

Those suckers have no idea what they're missing down here, I thought. *They probably can only imagine what it must be like to be untethered from society, living on these remote islands.*

I hadn't even once thought of picking up my smart-phone since I'd left the boat. Not that I could do much with it, hundreds of miles away from the nearest wi-fi signal. I glanced over at Teuila, who was rubbing my cargo shorts with a taro root amid a froth of white foam in the shallows near the beach. She looked up at me and smiled in my direction.

"Are you starting to feel better?" she called. "Don't stray too far from the beach. There are treacherous currents near the reef. The last thing we need is for you to drown after nursing you back to health."

"Not to worry," I shouted. "I'm just enjoying this little moment of bliss."

After five minutes or so, I began to walk out of the water in Teuila's direction. As I emerged from the surf, she eyed my body from top to bottom. She seemed particularly inter-ested in my bare mound as her eyes danced over my pale

"I could do with a bite, but we didn't bring anything. What did you have in mind?"

"The island provides everything we need," she said, glancing up toward the canopy of trees. "How about some fresh pineapple?"

I looked up and saw a clump of spiny pods bunched together under the leafy umbrella of long green fronds at the top of the tree.

"I'd love some, but how can we get those down?"

Teuila smiled, as she rubbed the bottom of her feet.

"These tough soles are good for more than just *walking* over rough surfaces," she said.

She placed her adze on the ground, then approached one of the palm trees and grasped its cracked bark with two hands, placing the soles of her feet in perpendicular positions against the sides of the trunk. She pulled her body toward the trunk and lifted her feet a few inches higher, pointing her knees outward. Then she pressed upward with her legs, taking a higher handhold on the stem. After a series of similar shimmying maneuvers, it didn't take long for her to ascend halfway up the tree.

I shook my head, dumbfounded at how easily she could scale the timber using just her arms and legs. With her legs splayed apart, I could clearly see under her tunic, and my pussy began to water as I watched her buttocks and vulva flexing with each leapfrog up the tree. When she neared the crown, she looked down and called out to me.

"You might want to stand back a bit. I'm going to shake the tree now, which should drop a few pineapples. They're pretty sharp and prickly, so make sure you stay out of the way."

I nodded as I looked up at her, taking a few steps back. As she started shaking her body against the tree, the leaves white hips. As I approached her, she held open a painted native dress, and I stepped into it while she pulled it up over my breasts and fastened it with loose strings behind my shoulders.

"Do you mind my asking," she said, as I turned around to face her. "Why your *agava* is smooth like a young girl's? It seems strange to see a full-grown woman without any hair down there. Is this a particular custom of Euro—I mean *American*—women?"

"As a matter of fact," I chuckled. "It is. "It's become the norm for Western women to shave themselves down there. I'm not exactly sure how the practice started. Maybe it's because it makes us seem younger and more alluring to our sexual partners. Or maybe it's just easier to navigate around down there. I find it heightens the sensation when I'm touched in that delicate area. But I can see how strange that must seem to someone who's used to living a natural lifestyle."

"Actually," Teuila said, thinning her eyelids as she peered at my deep cleavage atop the tight-fitting tunic. "I find it quite sexy. You look like a doll. A very curvy and *sexy* doll."

"I've never been called that before, but I'll take it as a compliment." I glanced in the direction of the village. "When does the festival start? What can I do to help you prepare?"

"First of all, we need to get you properly dressed for the festivities. The ceremony will start at dusk. Let's go back to my hut and see if we can make you look like a proper Anutian girl."

I paused for a moment, raising my eyebrows in curiosity.

"Is that the name of your island—*Anuta*?"

"Yes. It means slippery shore. Because our island is so small and far away from anybody, everything seems to just slide by us."

That's not the only thing that's slippery right now, I thought, feeling the cool sea breeze wafting over my bare vulva as I watched Teuila's sexy lips moving.

When we got back to her hut, Teuila and her grandmother fitted me with a grass skirt and decorated my hair with a garland of native flowers. The old lady pinched her eyebrows when she saw my bare pubis and she ran the back of her hand over my mound, making a comment to Teuila about my lack of *lauulu.* I wished it had been the young girl who had caressed me instead, but I hoped we'd soon have an opportunity to explore each other when we alone later.

I found it interesting that they left the upper half of my body exposed, draping it simply with the long floral lei that her grandmother had brought into the hut earlier. The flower petals were bright and soft, and they tickled my nipples as they fell over the fullness of my breasts. I smiled at the old woman and nodded in appreciation as she pulled it over my neck.

"What's your grandmother's name?" I asked Teuila.

"Her given name is *Tausa'afia,* meaning kind one, but we all call her Nona."

"You Anutians seem to prefer long and difficult-to-pronounce names. Does your grandmother have a pet name for you?"

"She calls me Te', like the French word for tea."

"That's perfect," I said, "because you're both so kind and calming."

I looked at the old woman and smiled, caressing the floral lei gently between my fingers.

"Thank you, Nona," I said, "for this lovely gift. You've both made me feel so welcome in your home. I'm looking forward to tonight's celebration."

6

Shortly after dusk, Teuila and her grandmother escorted me out to the main promenade of their village. A huge bonfire was burning at one end while her father sat on an elevated platform at the opposite end. Nona sat on the right side of the chief's platform along with his younger sons, while Te' and I sat on his left side with her sisters. This was the first time I'd seen her entire family assembled in one place, and I counted a grand total of eight siblings, all considerably younger than Teuila. Arrayed in front of us on a long serving plank were huge bowls and plates made of seashells festooned with a variety of fragrant foods. The rest of the villagers sat in family units on opposite rows lining the central esplanade, eyeing me curiously.

Further to the side of the chief's platform stood two men dressed in grass skirts with woven mats on their chests, wearing what looked to be war paint on the sides of their cheeks. In front of them rested hollowed-out logs with an animal skin pulled tightly over the top, while they held two large bones in each of their hands. When all the families had taken their designated seats, the chief raised his arm and a hush fell over the assembly.

"Amata le pati!" he hollered, nodding toward the two drummers flanking his platform.

The drummers started beating their drums rhythmically, and everyone began singing and chanting in their native dialect while the young women of each family stood to assemble in the central square. Teuila squeezed my hand, then stood up to join the other girls in the pit. As the older women began singing in their heavily accented intonation, the girls in the square began swinging and shaking their hips in rhythm with the beat. I watched in fascination as they swiveled their perfectly toned bodies to the music. Their grass skirts shimmied suggestively as their bare stomachs and breasts writhed under the skimpy covering of their flowery leis.

This was the first time I'd seen Teuila's pretty figure partially unclothed since the waterfall, and my eyes widened as I watched her sexy hips swaying to the music. She had virtually no fat on her immaculately toned stomach, and my mouth watered watching her abdominal muscles twitching and flexing on her tanned midriff. Knowing she was naked under her heavy straw skirt made the display all the more intoxicating, and I began to shake my own hips on the ground, as much in sympathy with the dancers as to produce some much-needed friction on my acting clit.

After a few minutes, Te' pointed at me and curled her finger in a come-hither manner, motioning for me to join the girls in their hula dance. I looked at her with a quizzical expression shaking my head, but she danced closer to me and held out her hand for me to stand up. I looked at the other women sitting around the square as they continued singing, and they smiled and nodded at me, encouraging me to join the group. I was still feeling a bit dizzy and sore, but I knew this was an opportunity I'd regret if I didn't take part.

I clasped Te's hand and walked with her toward the other dancers, trying to mimic the shaking of their hips like I did when I was a little girl trying to balance a hula hoop. It felt awkward trying to match the vigor and pace of their movements, and as I joined the line, the older women around the camp smiled at me with big grins. Whether they were simply trying to contain their mirth at the awkward attempts of the European woman attempting to mimic their native dance technique, or they were just happy to see me joining in with the rest of the locals in the celebration, was unclear. I looked up at the chief resting on the platform, and he nodded approvingly at my awkward attempt to dance an authentic tribal hula.

At least I can blame my rubbery legs on the after-effects of the snake venom, I thought.

After ten minutes or so, I began to feel wobbly, and I motioned to Teuila that I needed to sit down. She nodded and escorted me back to our resting position, holding my hand as she continued shimmying her hips to the music. When the song ended, the hula girls sat down with their families, and a group of young men carrying long spears stood to take opposite positions in two straight lines facing one another about five feet apart.

As the drummers began beating their drums more vigorously, the two men at the far end of the line moved into the center row and began dancing in a side-step fashion toward the front of the line, thrusting their spears forward and back in a menacing fashion. The combination of their fierce expressions and scary war paint, along with the waving of their stone-tipped spears, certainly looked convincing to me. I wondered what purpose these warrior actors could find for their threatening weapons in what appeared to be an otherwise peace-loving culture.

When the two men from the back of the line reached the front, they took positions beside their compatriots in the straight lines, stomping the bottom of their spears on the ground as the next pair at the end of the line copied their routine. In this manner, the line of warriors slowly but steadily approached closer to the chief's platform and our own position. As the drumming and chanting slowly built toward a crescendo, Teuila squeezed my hand as if to assure me that the spectacle was all for fun.

But I noticed as the final pair of dancers approached the front of the line that the tallest and most imposing one kept his eyes locked on Teuila the whole time. When he reached the end of the line, he bellowed some kind of war chant and glanced down at the two of us holding hands, then he took his position at the front of the formation, closest to the chief.

"That one seems to have a special interest in you," I whispered to Teuila, trying not to stare at his scary expression.

"I think he has designs on me," Te' nodded. "Manaia's been following me around the village the last few months. I've caught him and my father having private chats whenever I return from the women's lagoon."

"Well he certainly looks like a *capable* mate," I said, noticing the young man flexing his arm and leg muscles as he stared at us.

"That's exactly what I'm afraid of," Teuila said as she passed me some fresh plates of fish and manioc from the buffet table in front of us. "But for now, let's not fret about what may be. Let's enjoy the moment and savor all the good food and dancing."

7

After the ceremony ended, Teuila's family returned to their small hut, where we all slept shoulder-to-shoulder on the dusty floor. I wanted to reach out and touch her lying next to me, but her father's heavy breathing so close by soon squelched my desire. In the morning, we all shared a hearty breakfast of frigate eggs, yams, and fermented breadfruit paste on the porch overlooking the courtyard. As I gobbled up the savory mix of yolk-stained starch and sour mash, I marveled at how tasty the local cuisine was in the absence of our typical Western condiments.

Later that morning, Teuila led me on a private tour of the island. As we traipsed into the heavy brush along a stony path, I shook my head wondering how she could cover such rough ground in bare feet. The only thing she carried with her was a stone adze which she used to hack away the overhanging leaves, and the one-piece dress on her back made from pressed bark.

"Be careful with that thing," I said, following her a few feet behind. "We don't want to antagonize another one of those tree snakes. I'm not sure I could carry you back to the village like you did for me if you get bitten."

"Don't worry about me," Teuila said. "I've acquired a certain degree of immunity. Our people believe that all living things are endowed with supernatural powers—what we call *mana*. We've learned to live in harmony with our fellow island dwellers. As long as we leave them alone, they shouldn't cause us too much trouble."

"Tell that to the critter who bit me by the waterfall. I don't think he's recognized my mana yet."

"Never fear," Te' chuckled, "Worst-case scenario, I can always resuscitate you with my special potion."

"Mmm, yes," I said, remembering our last kiss. "In that case, bring on all the angry serpents you can find."

As I watched her scamper over the jagged rocks and thick brush lining the trail, I glanced at her soiled feet.

"How can you walk over all this rough terrain in bare feet?" I asked. "I'm wearing heavy hiking shoes, and I'm already feeling sore and all scratched up."

"The soles of our feet get pretty toughened up from all the coarse surfaces we walk on from the moment we're born. Between the sandy beaches, the rocks in the lagoon, and rough brush in the jungle, we soon develop a thick skin to protect us against most obstacles. But if you need to rest for a moment, there's a clearing up ahead where we can stop for a bite to eat."

"I could use a little respite," I nodded, breathing heavily from the steep uphill climb. "I'm a little out of shape from all the lounging around I've been doing since I began my tour of these Pacific islands."

We stopped at a small clearing surrounded by a copse of tall palm trees.

"Are you hungry?" Te' asked.

began rustling and a few seconds later four or five pineapples plopped to the ground beside me. She descended the
tree just as easily as she'd climbed it, and when she got to
the bottom, she rubbed the loose bark off her hands then
brushed the debris covering the front of her gown.

"Now I see why you native girls wear such thick clothing," I said, pinching her cloth between my fingers. It felt a
bit like thin cardboard, though it clung to her curvy figure
like a cotton dress.

"The bark of the mulberry tree is like papyrus," she said.
"And it's easy to decorate using turmeric dye and volcanic
mud. Nothing goes to waste on our island."

I picked up one of the spiny pineapples off the ground
and held it in my hand, feeling its heavy weight.

"These look pretty nutritious. But how will we get to the
flesh inside?"

"It's simple with the right tools," Teuila said, taking the
fruit from my hand.

She placed the husk against the side of the tree, then
deftly hacked the two ends off with her sharp adze. Then
she chopped the shell in half across the middle and placed
the two hollow rings against the trunk and cut each section
into two semi-circular crescents. We sat down, leaning our
backs against the tree, and bit into the juicy pulp like water-
melon pieces. The yellow juice squirted all over my face as I
bit into it, running down my chin. I drew the back of my
hand across my mouth, then wiped the sticky juice on the
blanket of leaves lining the forest floor.

"Be careful there," Teuila said, noticing the juice drib-
bling down my neck toward my T-shirt. "Or we'll have to do
another load of wash."

She rubbed her fingers over my chest just above my
cleavage then sucked her fingers into her mouth.

"Anything to get me out of my clothes again near you," I said, feeling my pussy throb from her seductive gesture. "Besides, I can always change into my new native garb," remembering how sexy I felt wearing just a grass skirt and floral lei around my neck.

"We might be able to get you out of those clothes and cleaned up sooner than you think," Te' said, motioning further up the trail. "There's another waterfall about twenty minutes up the slope, with a secluded swimming hole. It's one of my favorite places to go when I want to be alone."

"To convene with nature or to find some private play time?" I said, raising an eyebrow.

"Both. But this time, we won't just have to *watch* each other."

"Mmm, yes," I said, feeling my panties moistening with a different kind of juice. "I've been dreaming of touching you ever since I laid eyes on you two days ago."

"We better get a move on then," Te' said. "Because I'm definitely starting to feel hot under the collar."

Teuila and I quickly finished eating our pineapple slices, then we continued walking up the trail. As I watched her sexy hips rocking back and forth in her tight native smock, I reflected back to the ceremony last night and her extended family sleeping on the floor of their straw hut.

"Do you mind my asking," I said. "Whatever happened to your mother? Your grandmother is so sweet and helpful, but with such a large family, how do you and your father manage?"

"She died many years ago when she stepped on a rusty knife a European traveler had left on the beach and her foot became septic. The infection spread rapidly, and we had no way of saving her. I think this is one of the reasons why my father is so suspicious of Western visitors."

"I'm so sorry to hear that. Did your father ever remarry? I noticed that most of your siblings are quite a bit younger than you."

"He never quite recovered emotionally from her loss. But our tribe has a culture of sharing between families, and he's adopted many children whose mothers and fathers died during fishing expeditions and other natural disasters."

"So your Nona raised you from the time you were young? Where did you learn to speak such good English?"

"There was a period when my father welcomed the presence of Western visitors. We had a missionary school set up for many years where other children of my age studied many of the same subjects you learn in primary school. But my father became suspicious of their motivation after a period of time and banished them from our island, fearful they were stealing his *mana*. Ironically, they might have been able to save my mother if he'd allowed them to stay."

"It's a difficult proposition," I nodded, "melding two disparate cultures. Many other native people around the world have rejected Western help for the same reasons. It's never easy for men to relinquish the reins of power, no matter how much his subjects may welcome the change."

"My father can be a stubborn man," Te' said. "But his heart's in the right place. Even though our tribespeople defer to him, our culture of *aropa* dictates that all of our natural spoils be shared equally by the community. He's never tried to hoard resources or oppress our people in any direct way."

"What about this cargo ship that visits the island from time to time?" I said, reflecting back on his order that I leave the island as soon as practicable. "Why does he still permit the occasional outside intrusion?"

"We only exchange *goods* when the ship comes around,"

Teuila explained. "The markets in Honiara on the Solomon Islands are willing to pay a high price for the shark fins we harvest. We barter their equivalent value for things like nylon fishing line, cloth sails, and nets for catching fish in the lagoon."

"*Shark fins?*" I said, cringing at the thought of sharks flapping helplessly in the sea without their essential means of navigation.

"Don't worry," Te' said. "We use every part of the fish we catch. Shark flesh is considered a delicacy in our tribe. We even use their teeth as cutting blades."

"Nothing goes to waste," I nodded, breathing a sigh of relief.

After another twenty more minutes of hiking, I began to hear the sound of a cataract in the distance, and before long we came upon a break in the forest with a small waterfall cascading into a shallow pool.

"Do you feel like cooling off?" Teuila said, smiling toward me.

"Do I ever," I said, practically tearing my clothes off.

As I watched Te' step out of her one-piece tunic, I studied her body carefully. I hadn't seen her fully naked since the last time we were near a waterfall, and I could feel my nipples hardening as I ran my eyes all over her athletic figure. Her breasts sat up firm and high on her chest, and her dark teats stood out prominently on her caramel-colored skin. As she wiggled out of her tight dress, I couldn't help staring at the triangle-shaped patch of dark pubic hair nestled between her exquisitely carved hips.

"You look like you've never seen a naked woman before," Te' laughed, noticing me soaking up her body.

"Just not one so naturally pretty," I said.

"Come on," she said, standing on the edge of an abutment overlooking the aquamarine pool. "How do you Americans say it? Last one in is a rotten egg!"

Teuila placed her arms over her head then executed a perfectly clean dive into the murky water. Before she could surface, I chickened out and jumped off the cliff, placing my hands between my legs to protect the slap of water against my private parts. When we both surfaced, we splashed and squirted water towards each other's faces, giggling like little girls. I swam toward her and wrapped my arms around her back, pressing our chests together as our mouths joined in blissful union. As we kicked our legs together under the surface to stay afloat, our hips bumped together and I could feel her bush rubbing against my bare mound. The more passionate our kiss became, the harder it became for the two of us to stay above the water.

"Come," Teuila smiled, motioning toward the waterfall. "Let's go somewhere more comfortable. I bet you've never experienced a true Anutian shower before."

We swam to the base of the waterfall, then climbed up over the slippery rocks and ducked our heads under the chute. As we pressed our bodies together under the torrent, I leaned down and sucked Te's nipples into my mouth. She placed her hands behind my head and pulled me closer, purring under the falling water. I slowly kissed my way back up her chest and thrust my tongue deep into her mouth, kissing her passionately.

As our tongues danced in each other's mouths, we ran our hands over each other's bodies. I reached behind Te's back and cupped her firm buttocks in my palms, and she pressed her mound tightly against mine. I pulled away just far enough to slip my hand between the front of her thighs and began to stroke her slippery lips, pressing my fingers gently inside her. She spread her legs further apart and I drew my hand over her soft bush, pinching her clit softly between my two fingers.

As Teuila began moaning in my mouth, I rubbed my fingers in gentle circles around her nub. It only took a few moments before her hips to begin shaking as she gasped into my ear. I held her tightly against me, rubbing our nipples together, as she experienced her first orgasm at the hand of another woman.

8

Teuila and I made love on the grassy knoll overlooking the waterfall then slept under the late afternoon sun to dry off. By the time we woke up, it was already starting to get dark and we headed back to the village, walking hand-in-hand along a moonlit beach. It felt sublime to take my shoes off and feel the warm seawater lapping at our feet as we talked about our past experiences and future plans. But as we neared her village, Te' suddenly became quiet.

"Is everything alright?" I asked, fearing she was having second thoughts about our making love. "Are you angry with me for taking advantage of you at the waterfall?"

"No, Jade," she said, smiling warmly into my eyes. "It was beautiful. I'm so glad you were my first. I can't imagine a more tender and giving lover."

"You seem a little pensive. Was there something on your mind?"

"It's just—", Te' paused, as she looked out over the moonlight reflecting off the ocean. "I know you'll be leaving soon.

I've grown fond of you in the short time we've been together. I can't imagine being alone on this island without you."

I paused and ran my hand softly through her hair.

"As you said earlier, you're hardly alone here. You've got a loving family and the support of your entire community. I've rarely seen the kind of mutual love and generosity practiced by your tribe. Your tradition of aropa is a rare and wonderful thing."

"It's true that we all get along and share everything communally," Teuila said. "But what you and I have is something personal and special. I've never felt this way with someone else before. You make my heart dance."

I placed my arms around Te's shoulders and held her gently as I watched the surf crash softly against the shore. I was surprised by how close I'd grown to her in the three days we'd been together. But I worried that her feelings were being influenced by her youth and inexperience. I remembered what it felt like to fall in love the first time and how fragile our relationship was as my high school sweetheart and I took our first steps into the adult world.

"Oh Te'," I said, cradling her face in my hands. "I feel the same way about you. But we have to be careful about letting our emotions get carried away. We have such a short time together. I think we should just live in the moment and enjoy this while it lasts."

Teuila looked at me with a pained expression as a tear rolled down her cheek.

"Why can't you take me *with* you?" she pleaded. "The missionaries have taught me so much about the outside world. I think it would be so exciting to live with you in America."

I paused for a long moment as my eyes traced back and forth across her pretty face. She'd broached a subject both of us had fantasized about, but up until now neither of us had had the courage to express.

"How would that work?" I said. "America is thousands of miles away, both geographically and culturally. It would be a huge adjustment for you. And besides—I'm not sure your father would allow it. You're his only natural child, and you've already told me how suspicious he is of Western people."

Even though I was trying to talk her out of the crazy idea, I was already thinking about how I might arrange her landed immigrant status. The island of Anuta had no sovereign status as an independent nation and there were no embassies or consulates to help prepare the necessary paperwork. How could I even prove that she'd reached the age of majority?

"I'm a grown woman!" Teuila shouted. "I'm old enough to make my own decisions. Some of the young men from our island have traveled aboard the cargo ship in the past to pick up provisions in Honiara. My father can't stop me if I want to explore the world. And there's no one I'd rather do it with than you."

I pulled her close to me and held her tightly, feeling her heart beating against mine. It was an audacious idea, but not an insurmountable one. Surely there must be a protocol in place for allowing people from unrecognized jurisdictions into the United States. Even if I had to *marry* her—"

I pulled myself back and placed my hands on Te's shoulders. I couldn't believe I was thinking the unthinkable.

"Let's sleep on this tonight and talk about it in the morning, okay? This is all happening so fast. I don't want you to do something you'll regret later. We've still got a couple of weeks to explore our feelings for one another and talk to your father to test his receptivity to this idea."

I glanced over in the direction of the village and noticed a billow of white smoke rising into the night sky.

"Let's head back to your hut. He's probably worried about you. Like you said, we shouldn't test his patience too quickly."

"Yes," Te' sighed. "He's probably thinking about sending out a search party if we don't return soon." She clasped my arms firmly, furrowing her brow. "Promise me that you'll think about this. I want to be with you forever."

I looked into her limpid brown eyes and smiled.

"I promise," I nodded.

As we continued strolling through the foamy surf, I suddenly felt my own heartbeat pounding strongly in my chest.

Forever's a long time, I thought.

When we returned to Te's village, everyone was already lying asleep on the floor of her hut. Her father was reclining in a rocking chair on the front veranda with his eyes closed, snoring loudly. We crept up the front stairs and passed by him as he snorted, then we took off our clothes and pulled a taro blanket over us, reclining in the far corner next to some of the young children. We tried to sleep, but we were both still too excited about what had happened at the waterfall and about our discussion on the beach.

Te' rolled over on her side and pressed her hips against mine, and we mashed our mounds together, sighing quietly in each other's mouths. It was difficult to remain quiet with the sound of our moving bodies on the crunchy mats underneath us, but once our clits joined together, we couldn't stop tribbing one another until we both reached a powerful climax together. Five minutes later, Te's father rose from his chair on the porch and paused in the doorway for a long time, watching the two of us lying peacefully next to one another. When he finally lay down on the other side of the cabin and began snoring, we giggled under the covers and fell asleep in each other's arms.

We woke up to the sound of Te's siblings chattering on the front porch and got dressed, finding Nona preparing breakfast. The chief was nowhere to be found, but a few minutes later I noticed him talking privately at the far end of the courtyard with the young man who'd shown such an intense interest in Te' at the feast two nights ago. When her father approached the hut, he looked at Te' with a serious expression and motioned with his head for her to join him in the courtyard.

I watched the two of them walk down the sandy esplanade together, then Teuila suddenly stopped as she confronted her father with a raised voice. I heard the chief mention something about Manaia, and Te' shook her head violently, gesturing wildly with her hands. Shortly after, she stomped up the path and grabbed my hand, leading me into the woods.

"What is it, Te'?" I asked. "Was your father angry that we returned so late last night?"

"Worse," she said as tears streamed down her cheeks. "Much worse. He heard us making love last night and disapproves of how close we've become. He intends to marry me to Manaia in a ceremony tomorrow night."

9

—————

That night, neither one of us slept well. I kept replaying the image of Teuila being violated by her groom as she fought to resist his advances. I could feel her tossing and turning next to me, and whenever she cried out or whimpered in her sleep, I cradled her gently in my arms. My mind raced with crazy ideas of stealing one of the tribe's canoes and sailing to safety to the nearest neighboring island. But I no idea in which direction that might be, and neither Teuila nor I had any way of navigating our way through the open seas. Even if the charter boat crew returned for me, it wouldn't be easy to kidnap the chief's daughter from the clutches of her heavily armed tribe. After running every possible scenario through my head, I eventually fell asleep resigned to the idea that my precious island girl would soon be wrenched away from me.

In the morning, Nona began preparing a special meal for the evening's ceremony while some of Te's sisters braided her hair under the watchful eye of her father. We were both under virtual house arrest, with the chief posting an armed guard outside the front door of their hut. He wasn't taking any chances that the two of us might steal away again before his daughter was betrothed to Manaia. Te' put on a brave face as her sisters talked excitedly with her, but she kept glancing toward me with sad eyes. Fortunately, we were the only ones in her family who spoke English, so at least we were able to carry on a limited discussion.

"You look beautiful," I said, peering at her pretty face with her hair pulled back behind her head. "I like you in braids."

"The girls have lots of practice," Te' frowned. "With all the mats and baskets they've woven, they could probably do this with their eyes closed." She looked at her grandmother scraping some manioc shavings into a large wooden bowl. "That and cooking is pretty much all we women do around here."

I glanced at Teuila's father, who was sitting cross-legged on the other side of the hut, watching us with a stern expression.

"What about raising a *family*?" I said. "Isn't that something you're looking forward to? You and your sisters seem to have a close relationship."

"Jade," Te' said, shaking her head slowly. "I know you're trying to make me feel better, but it's no use. You're the only one I want. There's nothing else in the world that I need as long as I'm with you."

I tightened my lips, trying to hold back my emotions.

"It won't be so bad," I said. "Lots of marriages are arranged. Over time, I'm sure you'll grow to love your new husband. After I'm gone, you'll soon forget about me—"

"I could *never* forget you," she said, her eyes flaring. "And I'll never love that brute. As long as we're apart, I'll never be happy."

"Te'," I said, glancing in her father's direction. "We have

to accept the reality of the situation. It's out of our hands now. You'll soon be married, we'll be separated from each other, and I'll be banished from the island. It's best that you get on with your life..."

"I've been thinking," she said. "There might be another way. All we have to do is find a way to get the two of us away from the clutches of my father for a few moments. Then we can slip into the forest and hide away until one of the boats comes to pick you up."

I glanced at the two burly men standing opposite the front steps of their hut holding sharp spears in their hands.

"How could we do that? Your father doesn't seem to want either one of us out of his sight, much less *both* of us at the same time."

"It shouldn't be too difficult to stretch your legs for a moment. It's me that he's primarily worried about. He knows you couldn't fend for yourself very long if you ran away. He'd probably be *happy* if something were to happen to you, so I'd stop pining for you. We just need to find a way to get you out of the hut. Then all I'd need to do is create a distraction and slip away. I know this island better than anyone. There are lots of places where we could hide out for a few weeks."

"I don't know, Te'," I said. "It sounds risky. What if we get caught? Your father doesn't seem like the kind of man to let that sort of challenge to his authority go unpunished. There's no rule of law on this island. It wouldn't take much for him to have me put down. I have a feeling he's already at the end of his patience."

Teuila paused for a long moment as her eyes studied my face. As much as I was concerned for my own safety, I was far more worried about the consequences to *her* if we got caught. The worst thing would be for her to see me tortured or killed for disrespecting the chief's power.

"Do you think you could find your way back to the waterfall we visited yesterday?" she asked.

"I don't know, maybe. I suppose if I followed the same path—"

"If you can find your way there, I'll meet you in a couple of hours. Worst-case scenario, you can hide out in the jungle and live off pineapples and taro root until your ship arrives. My father won't harm you with other Westerners around. He knows it would just bring more visitors to the island and threaten his position as chief."

I shook my head and sighed heavily.

"But on what pretense would he let me out of the hut? And what if he sends an armed guard with me? How would I escape?"

Te' paused as her eyes darted from side to side.

"We'll need to relieve ourselves eventually. My father isn't such a brute that he'd insist on our doing our business right here on the floor of the hut. You can ask to be escorted to the women's bathing lagoon, then ask the guard to let you take care of business behind a clump of palm trees. When his back is turned, do you think you could climb to the top of one of those trees like I showed you? He'll never expect you to do that, searching the trails and beach for your foot-prints, not looking up."

I closed my eyes, reflecting back on Te's technique climbing the pineapple tree. She'd made it look remarkably easy, and I was still in decent shape from my regular trips to the gym.

"I think so. But how long will I have to stay up there before it's safe to come down?"

"My guess is that if the guard can't find you within a few

minutes, my father will tell everyone to forget about you. He'll be far more concerned about letting me out of his sight."

"And how will you manage that?"

"Let *me* worry about that," Te' smiled. "I'm very resourceful. Just make sure you find your way back to the waterfall. It's a big island, and it will be very difficult to find each other again if you get lost."

"I can't believe I'm considering this," I said, feeling my heart beginning to pound in my chest.

For the first time in many years, I'd never felt so alive. The idea of running away from an angry tribe on an isolated island with the girl of my dreams was beyond any fantasy I'd ever imagined. I could feel the adrenaline coursing through my veins and the hairs on the sides of my arms standing on end.

"I'm in," I said.

Teuila turned to speak with her father for a few moments, then he paused as he appraised my demeanor. I tried to remain as calm as possible, but I could feel the veins in my neck pulsing like crazy as he glared at me. Eventually, he gave a single nod of his head, then rose to give instructions to one of the guards standing outside the front door.

"*Alu*," he said to me, jerking his head towards the open door. "*Le maua manatu.*"

"What did he say?" I asked Teuila.

"Pretty much what we expected. He's going to send a guard with you who won't give you a lot of space to maneuver, so you'll have to choose your position carefully. Find one with enough cover to protect your modesty, but also close enough to a tree so that you can climb it without him noticing you. I'll come for you as soon as I can."

"Be careful," I said, standing to exit the cabin.

"You too."

I paused at the door of her hut and looked back at Teuila one last time. I didn't know if or when I'd see her again.

When I got to the base of the front steps, one of the guards looked sternly at me then motioned with his spear in the direction of the women's lagoon. As I walked down the same sandy path where all the tribespeople had welcomed me so warmly two nights ago, I noticed the women and children tracing my movement with vacant expressions.

It looks like I'm on my own again, I thought.

When we reached the edge of the lagoon, the guard motioned to a shallow depression at the edge of the brush.

"*Oe alu ai*," he ordered, pointing to the basin with his spear.

I glanced around the area, noticing there was little surrounding vegetation to provide privacy for someone taking care of such intimate business.

I shook my head as I pulled on my shorts, indicating that I needed more privacy. He looked around the edge of the lagoon and pointed to a more secluded spot about a hundred feet up the beach, next to a small clump of coconut trees. When we reached the spot, I climbed behind a small bush and began to squat, noticing the guard still watching me.

I motioned with my hand for him to look away, and he turned his back briefly. Knowing I'd only have a few seconds to act, I removed my hiking shoes and hid them in the brush. Then I crawled behind the sandy embankment toward the nearby palm trees. When I reached the furthest one, I stood and peered around the side of the trunk. The guard had turned around and was glancing curiously in the direction of the pit, tilting his head high in the air as he lifted his heels off the ground. He shouted something in his native language, and when I didn't respond, he rushed forward with a look of alarm, finding the pit empty.

He swiveled his head quickly from side to side, then peered at the stand of trees. As he began walking in my direction, I placed the soles of my feet against the side of the trunk as Teuila had shown me, then I grasped the crusty bark and pulled myself upward. As I heard the guard's footsteps nearing the stand, I began slowly shimming myself up the tree. With most of my weight borne by the inward pressure of my feet pressed against the trunk, it was easier than I expected to scale the thick stem. But as I pulled my knees inward, worrying he'd see them sticking out from the side of the tree, I ended up using more arm strength than I intended to move upward.

By the time I reached the crown of the tree and glanced down, I was sweating profusely. My feet were bleeding from the sharp crust pressing into my tender skin, but I was able to leverage my weight with tight handholds against the layered bark. As the guard peered frantically from side to side looking for me, I noticed the pod of coconuts under the palm fronds shaking precariously. Just as one of them snapped from its stem, I reached out and caught the husk as it fell into my open palm.

The guard cocked his head hearing the sound and started to look up. I threw the nut as far as I could in the direction of the bush, and when he heard it land in the dense thicket, he took chase into the forest. I sat in my cramped position breathing heavily as sweat poured down the front of my T-shirt, listening carefully for the sound of the guard's footsteps in the jungle. When the footfalls diminished into the distance, I quickly descended the tree, falling sharply to the ground. I looked around to make sure the way was clear, then I hobbled toward the far end of the beach and disappeared into the thick brush.

Half a mile away, Teuila sat patiently on the floor of her hut as her sisters finished decorating her hair with scented frangipani blossoms. She glanced toward her grandmother preparing the wedding ceremony dishes on the front veranda and asked her father if she could help. The chief nodded and followed Te' out onto the porch, taking a position in the rocking chair as he nodded toward the remaining guard.

Teuila sat next to her grandmother and Nona smiled, handing her a knife and a taro root to peel. Suddenly, the other guard came running up to the front of the hut, and when he told the chief that the white woman had escaped, her father summoned a group of young tribesmen and they ran off in the direction of the lagoon. Nona glanced at Teuila, pinching her eyebrows in suspicion, wondering what kind of trouble the girls were getting into now.

Te' picked up the taro root and smiled, remembering how Jade had teased her when she first bit into it. Suddenly, the vegetable slipped in her hand and the knife cut a deep diagonal gash along the side of her index finger. As her hand began spurting blood all over the white gourd, Nona dropped what she was doing and motioned for the guard to summon the village's medicine man. When the guard hesitated remembering the chief's orders to keep a close watch on his daughter, Nona screamed at him, warning that if Teuila was not attended to soon, she could suffer the same fate as her mother.

"Do you want to be responsible for the death of the

chief's daughter on the eve of her wedding?" she shouted in their native language.

The guard mumbled something and took off scurrying down the path. Nona looked at Te's cut shaking her head, then she wrapped a banana leaf around the wound and peered into her granddaughter's eyes.

"This wasn't an accident, was it?" she said.

"Forgive me, Nona," Te' said. "I love her. This is the only way I can be with her. Can you help me?"

Nona glanced down the sandy courtyard, then escorted Teuila toward the rear of their cabin, where she lifted a flap of leaves and pointed into the forest.

"*Lau manamea*," she said. "Be with your lover. I'll pray that you both find happiness. Go quickly now, before your father returns."

As Teuila scampered into the forest holding the green bandage tightly against her swollen finger, she yelped in glee, knowing she'd soon be in the arms of the only person she ever truly loved.

10

When I got far enough away from the cluster of palm trees, I ducked into the bush and paused to get my bearings. From my new location, it would be difficult to find my way back to the waterfall. All I could remember was that it was about an hour's hike uphill in a roughly forty-five-degree angle from the village. But from my vantage point in the women's lagoon, it would be almost impossible to pick up the trail through the thick jungle. My only chance would be to double-back towards the village and hope that nobody saw me.

To make matters worse, my feet were sore and bleeding from climbing the rough palm tree. I thought taking my shoes off would help me to climb the trunk more quietly, but I hadn't counted on puncturing my skin in multiple places. And it would be too risky to try to return to the pit to retrieve them. Like it or not, I'd have to make my way back up to the waterfall in bare feet.

I shook my head at the irony of my predicament.

The only way to truly appreciate another culture is to immerse yourself in it, I reminded myself. *Well now I'm really going native. Let's see how quickly I can develop tough Anutian soles.*

I peered over the top of my sand dune to see if the coast was clear. I hadn't heard from the guard since he ran off into the jungle, but I knew it would be too risky to use the cover of the thick brush to find my way back to the village. The carpet of broken twigs and sharp rocks on the forest floor would just make my feet worse, and the rustling of leaves could draw attention to my position. My only chance would be to backtrack along the beach before he returned.

But just as I prepared to sprint down the beach, I noticed my guard running toward me from the direction of the village, along with the chief and a group of other young tribesmen. They paused at the location where I'd squatted, and it didn't take long for the chief to find my hiking shoes.

"*O a nei?*" he shouted, holding my shoes up in the air.

The guard shook his head in bewilderment, then pointed into the jungle in the direction where I'd thrown the coconut.

"*Ona mamao,*" the chief said, throwing my shoes far into the lagoon. "*Salalau solo!*" he said, gesturing into the jungle in multiple directions.

As the group fanned out into the thick brush, I waited for a few moments then dashed back along the beach in the direction of the village. Feeling my blistered feet burning in the hot sand, I hobbled my way across the lagoon, glancing into the bush for any sign of the tribesmen.

Maybe it wasn't such a bad idea taking my shoes off after all, I thought, watching the impressions my feet left in the sand. I'm the only one on this island with Western shoes. It would be a whole lot easier to track me from the unique tread they'd leave on the ground than with my bare feet.

I just hoped the blood from my soles wouldn't leave another type of trail.

When I got to the edge of the village, I crouched low behind the back of the huts lining the central promenade, trying to stay out of sight. Small children giggled as they ran across the courtyard, playing a game of tag. One of the boys ducked under the crawlspace of the cabin I was hiding behind, and I pulled myself up on the side of the hut, trying to conceal my legs. He glanced in both directions to see if the coast was clear, then scampered back across the court-yard behind another hut.

Great, I thought. *Just what I need right now. A bunch of kids playing hide and seek. At least they're showing me some good hiding spots.*

As I slowly made my way toward the far end of the courtyard, I paused when I saw the chief's hut. There was no armed guard outside the front door, and I peered inside the darkened interior for any sign of Teuila. Her grandmother was peeling vegetables on the front porch, and she glanced in my direction, noticing movement across the lane. We locked eyes and for a moment and I was afraid she'd call out. But instead, she placed her finger to her lips, then motioned with an open hand toward the trailhead at the end of the square.

She made it! I breathed a sigh of relief. *God bless that woman.* Maybe I had a friend in the village after all.

I crept past the remaining huts lining the square then dashed onto the trail and scampered up the familiar path leading to the waterfall. Once I was on the path, I recog-nized the familiar landmarks and made good time picking my way up the slope. Even though the brush was thick, I was far more worried about bumping into one of the chief's chase team than I was about encountering another tree snake. When I reached the pineapple tree clearing, I knew I was on the right track and I smiled remembering the sight of Te's pretty ass climbing the tree.

Soon, I thought, *I'll have her all to myself.*

Thirty minutes later, I heard the sound of the waterfall nearby, and I breathed in the fresh scent of the misty air wafting over the trees. I didn't know if it was because all my senses were on high alert being on the run, or if it was because my heart was pounding knowing I'd soon be back with Teuila, but everything around me suddenly seemed so much more *alive.* The flowers at the side of the trail looked prettier, the air smelled sweeter, and the birds chirping in the distance sounded happier.

For the first time in many years, I was madly, deliriously in love.

When I reached the waterfall, I looked around frantically for my island girl, but there was no sign of her. I furrowed my brow, puzzled why she'd have taken longer to reach our destination than I had. She appeared to have had a head start on me, and she should have been able to scale the uneven path much quicker than me, especially with my chafed feet. But seconds later, she broke through the heavy brush on the opposite side of the waterfall and rushed toward me.

"Thank God you made it!" she said, throwing her arms around me. "I was so worried about you."

"Our little trick worked," I nodded, tilting the underside of one foot up toward her. "Although it looks like it's going to take a little longer than we hoped for the soles of my feet to get properly toughened up."

Teuila looked at my scarred soles and shook her head.

"What happened to your shoes?"

"I thought it would be safer to climb the tree without

them. But it didn't take long for your father to find where I'd hidden them. I guess I'll be walking around barefoot like a real Anutian sooner than we thought."

Teuila chuckled as she squeezed my hand.

"It's probably better this way anyhow," she smiled. "Those treads would be visible a mile away."

"Why did you come up the other way?" I said, pointing to the direction of the jungle where she'd emerged.

"I wanted to throw my father off the trail," she said, pointing to the imprint of my boots on the muddy embankment. "But it won't take long for them to find us. We have to get out of here as soon as possible."

I noticed that the leaf wrapped around Te's index finger was dripping blood down her hand.

"What happened?" I said. "You're hurt!"

"It's just a flesh wound," she said. "It looks worse than it is. We'll be able to patch up our wounds when we get to safety."

Suddenly we heard the shouting of men's voices approaching our position. I looked at Teuila with terrified eyes.

"What should we do?" I said. "In which direction should we head?"

"There's no time for that," Te' said. "We have to *hide*. There's too many of them. They'll catch us too quickly."

"Where?" I said, looking around the clearing. "In the brush?"

Te' glanced around the glade, then peered into a still section of the pool furthest from the waterfall.

"How long can you hold your breath?" she said.

I looked at the surface of the pond for a moment, then back towards her.

"Not long in my present state," I said, feeling my chest

heaving up and down. "Between my elevated state of adrenaline and my fear of being caught, I can hardly catch my breath as it is."

"What if we fashioned some kind of breathing tube?" she said, peering at some bulrushes at the far end of the pond. "Do you think you could remain still under the water while our tribesmen search the area?"

"I suppose so. What did you have in mind?"

"Those reeds on the other side of the pond are hollow. Follow me, but try to step as much as possible on the rocks instead of the dirt. We don't want them to be able to trace where we're hiding."

Teuila took my hand and led me to a flattened section of the embankment where we tiptoed over the scattered rocks on the edge of the shore. Then she slipped into the water and pushed herself away from the shore.

"Be careful when you step into the pond," she said. "We don't want to make too much noise or stir up the mud around the bank where they could see where we entered the water. Quickly now—I can hear them getting closer."

I lowered myself into the water then I pushed myself gently away from the shore. Teuila led me to the other side of the pond, then she pulled a pocketknife out of a pouch on her tunic and cut two four-foot lengths of reed. She tested each tube by puffing through them, then handed one to me. I could hear the sounds of the men's voices rising in volume and the rustling of the brush very close by.

"Put this in your mouth then duck under the water about three feet. Don't go any lower than that or you'll choke if the other end dips beneath the surface. Then follow me toward the waterfall. The rippling current will help camouflage us in the depths."

I looked at Teuila with frightened eyes, then placed the

tube in my mouth and submerged under the water. After a brief moment of panic, I realized it wasn't so different from using a snorkel. I was scared using one of those at first too, but once I learned that I could breathe comfortably underwater, it didn't take long for me to relax. After I dropped a few feet, I opened my eyes and saw Te' submerge beside me. Then she took my hand and pulled me toward the churning undercurrent next to the waterfall.

When we reached the base of the cataract, I glanced up through the foaming water and noticed a group of half-naked tribesmen walking around the base of the swimming hole, pointing toward footprints in the ground. I looked toward Teuila fearfully, and she pumped her palm up and down, motioning for me to remain calm. Her dress was billowing underneath her, spreading out to her sides, and I worried the white sheen of the fabric would be noticeable from above. But she placed her hands between her legs in a Marilyn Monroe manner and pressed the gown downwards as her long black hair floated upwards.

I shook my head, smiling at the improbability of the situation. Only Teuila could make almost suffocating under water while a bunch of savages circled around us menacingly look sexy.

Suddenly, I noticed Manaia standing on the edge of the embankment, looking intently into the water. He walked around the edge of the pond, thrusting the dull end of his spear into the water, as if searching for something under the surface. When he reached the clump of reeds, he paused for a moment, then moved closer to the edge of the waterfall. Teuila's eyes widened as he got closer, and she motioned for us to move closer to the base of the cataract. She pinched her fingers around the base of the tube in her mouth then pulled them away quickly as she puffed her cheeks.

I glanced at her for a moment, then nodded my head in understanding. One of the first things I'd learned when using a snorkel was how to purge the water from the tube whenever I ducked under water. I took a deep breath in, then we paddled under the falling water as I felt the reed vibrating from the pressure of the deluge above us. When the we finally reached a calmer section near the embankment, I blew heavily out the tube, feeling the water passing upward through the reed, then I breathed deeply in. There was still a bit of water in the cylinder and I coughed suddenly, but after a few more frantic purges, I was able to breathe comfortably again.

As we treaded water trying to remain in a fixed position, we looked up through the gurgling surface. Manaia stared in our direction for a long moment, then he finally stepped back from the shore and joined the rest of his team on the cliff. Teuila's father motioned in the direction of the brush where she'd emerged earlier, then the group quickly dispersed. I kicked my legs toward the surface, but Te' reached out and grabbed my arm, motioning for me to stay submerged a little longer. About a minute later, Manaia reemerged at the edge of the abutment and turned his head to scan the surface of the lagoon, then he took off again into the forest. Teuila waited another five minutes, then she signaled that it was safe to resurface.

"Oh my God!" I said, looking at her with wide eyes. "That was *intense*. I was sure that Manaia had seen us. That was smart of you to wait until he'd left the second time."

"It's still not entirely safe," Teuila said. "I think we should wait here for another half hour or so. Once we know that they're not coming back, we'll have to find another place to hide. I want to put as much distance between us and the village as possible."

I circled my hands gently underwater as my eyes darted over her face.

"What about the beach where my charter boat came in? You said that was a good day's hike from your village. That should be the first place my crew will look for me if they return."

"That might work," Te' nodded. "But we'll have to be careful about staying too close to the shore. My father will probably send out another search party following the perimeter of the island by canoe. We'll scope out the area when we get there."

I kicked my legs excitedly, realizing we'd soon be alone again.

"Teuila," I said, throwing my arms around her, almost pulling both of us underwater. "I'm so happy we're together again. I could live in a *cave* with you if I had to."

"Let's hope your friends return for you soon," she said, peering nervously around the edge of the waterfall. "That might be the only safe place for us to hide soon if they don't."

11

Tequila dressed my wounds with the milky sap of a spongy plant, then she wrapped my feet in banana leaves to help quell the bleeding. After a few minutes, I could feel the pain and throbbing begin to subside, and I shook my head marveling at her ability to apply natural cures. But I was far more concerned about the cut on her finger, which was still dripping blood under her makeshift bandage.

"That feels better," I said, lifting her hand to take a closer look at her incision. "But your cut looks far worse. Will a couple of leaves will be enough to close that wound?"

"I missed the main artery," she said, squeezing her finger tenderly. "I just need to apply a tight compress to stem the bleeding and allow it to clot."

She glanced down at my wet T-shirt and smiled.

"Do you think you'd be willing to part with your shirt? If we tear it into strips, we can wrap it around both my finger and your feet. We've got a long walk ahead of us to get to the other side of the island and it will help keep the dirt out of your wounds."

"Why not?" I smiled. "I've done it once before already. Now that we're alone, I don't feel so self-conscious about protecting my modesty." I pulled my shirt over my head and handed it to her. "Do you want my bra too?"

Te' peered at my bosom pushed together with the constricting garment and shook her head.

"It's probably best that you keep that on for a little longer. There will be plenty of sharp objects poking out of the brush as we make our way through the jungle. We don't want to get those pretty breasts of yours all scratched up. Besides, we might be able to find a better use for it later."

She bit the bottom of my shirt to make a small incision, then tore it in half lengthwise down the front and the back before pulling off the sleeves. Then she hacked two narrow pieces of bark off a nearby tree with her adze and placed them under my feet, wrapping the long ends of my shirt around the husks and tying the ends firmly behind my ankle.

"Not quite as pretty as your Western shoes," she said, but hopefully they'll last at least until we get to the other side of the island.

I stood up and paced forward and back a few steps, testing my newly fashioned sandals.

"They're surprising comfortable," I nodded. "Especially with those leafy insoles. Maybe we can hook you up with Nike when we return to the States."

"Nike?"

"Just kidding," I laughed. "They're a big shoe manufacturer back home. You're a woman of many talents, Te'. I'm sure we can find you a more interesting job when the time comes."

Teuila looked up at me and smiled.

"I'm excited to learn all about your culture. But right

now, I think we should head over to the other side of the island. We don't want to overstay our welcome here. My father may come back to search for us if he doesn't find us elsewhere."

Teuila tore up one of the sleeves into a spiral strip, then she wrapped and tied it tightly around her wounded finger.

"Come on," she said. "Let's go see if we can find a better hiding place."

***

It took most of the day to cross to the other side of the island. Te' wanted to stay off the marked trails to avoid running into our search party, so we walked along the side of narrow creeks and streams to stay out of sight. I was afraid the stony riverbeds would splinter my makeshift moccasins, but the flexible bark absorbed most of the brunt and the shirt-tie miraculously survived the entire trip. When we passed the same waterfall where I was bitten by the snake, I knew we were getting close to the beach.

"How can you navigate through this dense jungle so easily?" I said, amazed at how she'd found her way back to the same spot on such a large island.

"I've lived here my whole life," she said. "I know this island like the back of my hand. There's not much else to do for fun around here, so I've made lots of expeditions in my eighteen years."

"I hope your father and your boyfriend don't know the island as well as you do. Otherwise, there'll be nowhere safe to hide."

"Don't worry about that," Te' said, peering up at the darkening sky. "I've had lots of practice hiding out in the forest. It's starting to get dark, so we won't have time to build a more comfortable shelter until the morning. We'll have to make do with a camouflaged lean-to for this evening. I'm looking forward to showing you how easily we can live off the land. We'll try to make the most of our little exile until your friends return."

"I'm looking forward to it too," I said, recalling my Robinson Crusoe fantasy. "This should be quite the adventure."

When we reached the beach where our charter boat had set anchor, Teuila checked out the lagoon and nodded.

"This will work fine. It's nicely secluded, has shallow water and shoals to catch fish, and has a good lookout for approaching boats."

"Where will we sleep?" I said, wrapping my arms around my chest, feeling the cool onshore breeze.

"It's probably best not to sleep on the beach tonight. My father may be sending out a canoe patrol to search the perimeter of the island. We'll have to sleep inland this evening."

I peered into Te's brown eyes and smiled.

"As long as lying I'm next to you, I can sleep anywhere."

Teuila found a secluded spot behind a sand dune and hacked down some large palm leaves to provide cover and keep us warm. Then she harvested a few pineapples and coconuts from some nearby palm trees, and we enjoyed an impromptu dinner.

"You must be hungry after trekking all day," she said, noticing me shivering as she placed some leaves over my bare torso. "Tomorrow we'll catch and cook up some fresh fish. But it's too risky to build a fire right now. Will you be warm enough sleeping here tonight?"

We lay down in the pit and Te' snuggled up close to me, pulling the big leaves over our bodies.

"I am *now*," I said, feeling her warm skin pressed against mine.

As much as I wanted to make love to her again, after ten hours of hiking we both fell asleep within minutes. In the morning, I woke to the sound of seabirds chirping in the distance as the morning sun began to warm up our little nest of leaves. Te' rolled over when I began to stir, and I kissed her gently.

"Did you sleep well?" I asked, caressing her warm shoulders.

"Like a log. But I had a few nightmares. I dreamed that my father found us and dragged us back to the village where he tied you to a stake in the main square. As everybody celebrated my marriage to Manaia, he set you aflame while I watched helplessly from his arms."

"Jesus!" I said, flaring my eyes open. "Would he actually *do* that if he caught us?"

"Perhaps not quite so viciously. But he's had other tribespeople punished for far less an offense."

Te' began lifting herself up to get out of the pit.

"We need to begin building fortifications and a better hiding place."

"Can't it wait a few more minutes?" I said, clutching her wrist. "This is the first time we've been alone in almost two days. I was hoping we could have a little fun before we get to work. Besides, don't you need to let your finger rest a little longer to let it heal?"

Teuila lifted her hand and untied the strip of cloth around her finger then opened the leaves to peer at her cut. The bleeding had stopped, but she had a nasty inch-long scar on the side of her hand.

"It still looks tender," I said, lifting her finger to my

mouth as I sucked on the tip gently. "Maybe it needs some of my special healing juices."

"I'm not sure it works that way," Te' chuckled. "But it feels good, just the same."

"Well if it feels good licking your *finger*, maybe I can make you feel even better licking you somewhere else."

I lifted Teuila's robe over her shoulders then lay her down on the leaves.

"Lie down while I give you some loving."

As I nibbled my way down the front of her chest, I cupped her firm breasts in my hands and sucked on her nipples. It felt sublime to be holding her in my arms for the first time, knowing she was truly mine. I swirled my tongue over her fleshy peaks, and she moaned in pleasure. I could feel her hips gyrating below me, and she gasped when I pressed my thigh against her opening.

While I continued to suck and nibble on her breasts, Teuila ground her pussy into my thigh, coating the front of my leg with her wetness. After a few minutes, I pulled away and drew my tongue over her quivering abdomen until I reached her furry mound. It had been eons since I'd seen or felt a full patch of pubic hair, and I paused as I caressed her soft fur.

"Mmm," I purred. "I love how soft you are down here. I could run my hands through your hair all day."

"I like the way you touch me, Jade," Te' panted. "Kiss my private areas. I want to feel your lips on my *agava*."

As I drew my face over her bush, I could feel the moisture from her pussy beading in her hairs. I closed my lips over her muff and lifted my head up a few inches, gently tugging her hair as I sucked her dew into my mouth. It might have just been my wild imagination channeling my

Blue Lagoon fantasy, but her juice tasted sweeter and fresher than anything I remembered.

The closer I got to her jewel, the harder she pushed her hips up into my mouth, and when I finally encircled her clit with my lips, she gasped out loud. As she spread her thighs further apart and I began to circle my tongue around her button, she began to whimper and call my name.

"Oh Jade," she whispered. "That feels so good. Lick me with your beautiful mouth. I want to feel you kissing me everywhere."

Hearing her cry out my name in the throes of passion sent a shiver down my spine, and I began to feel my own panties sticking to my skin. I wanted to feel her trembling against my face and call out my name as the waves of pleasure rolled over her. As her hips began shaking with increasing fervor, I sucked her into my mouth, dancing my tongue over her nub. When her hips began to rise up off the ground, I cradled her buns in my hands as she pressed herself tighter against my face.

"Yes, Jade," she groaned. "I can feel it coming now. Hold me while I release my *pito*. It's coming now!"

Suddenly, Te' growled as her hips began bucking wildly against my face and her buttocks started quivering in my palms. I opened my eyes and watched her tummy cavitating as she thrashed her head from side to side. I held her tightly while she spasmed against my face, coating me with her sweet, pungent syrup. When she finally stopped shaking, I lowered her hips to the cool leaves and snuggled up next to her.

"Does my healing touch work better that way?" I smiled, grinding my hips against her wet mound.

"Yes," she purred. "But now I think there's *another* wound that needs my attention."

Te' and I made love for the rest of the morning, then our growling stomachs reminded us how little we'd eaten in the last twenty-four hours.

"Come," she said, pulling me out of the pit. "Let's catch ourselves a proper breakfast, then we need to begin preparing a safer resting place. No more sleeping on the beach. I don't want to take any chances that my father and his thugs will stumble across us while we're resting. Let me show you how to catch fish the Anutian way."

She led me into the brush until we came upon a small stand of seedlings. Te' hacked two of them off near the base with her adze, then whittled the ends of each shoot down until they had sharp pointed ends.

I looked at her quizzically, wondering what she had in mind.

"Were you planning on using those in case we get ambushed?

"No, I would never harm my own people. These are for another type of creature. We're going to use them to spear fish."

"Really?" I said with wide eyes. "You can do that too? You really are a woman of many talents."

"It's not so easy to spear a free-swimming fish," she said. "But it's a lot easier when there's a bunch of them trapped in a contained area. That's where you come in. You're going to push them toward me."

"How will I do that?"

"You're going to rake them into a trapping area."

I pinched my eyebrows with a confused expression, and she smiled at me as she began chopping down a taller seedling. After she felled it, she chopped off the top to about a fifteen-foot length, then hacked off the branches on three sides so that it looked like a giant comb.

"That's a pretty big rake," I said.

"You'll find it works remarkably well at herding schools of fish into shallow water," Teuila said.

"How am I supposed to use it? It barely looks like I'll be able to lift that thing."

"I'll help you carry it to the shore. Then all you need to do is place the branch atop the water and push it up and down to scare the fish forward. I'll look after the rest. Are you ready?"

"Lead on, Pocahontas," I chuckled. "Show me your ways."

Teuila and I carried the big branch to the edge of the water, then we floated it to the far corner of the lagoon where we saw some schools of iridescent fish darting underneath the clear water.

"Those critters sure can scamper around down there," I said. "Are you sure we'll be able to snare one of them with just a spear?"

"Watch and learn, city girl."

Te' escorted me to a spot waist deep about twenty feet from the shore.

"I'm going to wade a little closer to the shore," she said. "When I signal that I'm ready, I want you to pump the pole up and down on the surface of the water as you slowly walk toward me. The sound and motion of the spikes pointing underwater will scare the fish in my direction. As they begin accumulating in the shallow water, it will make it easier for me to catch one."

When she got into position, Te' nodded toward me and I began to churn the water as she had instructed. Sure enough, within seconds a group of fish began flapping in her direction as they twisted and turned, confused by the agitating water. Some of them slipped around the ends of the rake, but enough moved forward that they began to congregate in the shallower water. When I got to within five feet of Teuila, she pulled one of the spears high above the surface and paused for a moment, then thrust it rapidly down into the water. Seconds later, she pulled the pole out of the depths with a flapping striped fish impaled on the end of the spike.

"Holy crap!" I said, hardly believing my eyes. "Is it that easy?"

"It takes a bit of practice. But it's a whole lot easier when you've got them bunched up in a narrow space."

"Here," she said, holding out the other spear to me. "Do you want to give it a try?"

"Okay," I said, wincing momentarily at the idea of killing such a pretty fish. But I loved my seafood, and catching a fish this way looked a whole lot less messy than using a hook and bait.

"Make sure you wait until you see a bunch of fish swimming near your feet," Te' said. "You don't have to aim at a single fish necessarily. It's a bit hit and miss. It might take you a few attempts to hit one. Just be careful you don't spear your own foot."

"No," I said, peering down at my still bandaged feet. "I think I've had enough scratched up feet for a little while, thank you. Just don't laugh at me."

"I wouldn't dream of it," Te' said.

As we took up our respective positions and Te' began scaring the fish toward me, I could see them darting underwater closer and closer to me. When she got close enough, she looked up and nodded.

"Now, Jade!" she yelled, as she pumped the surface of the water into a foamy brine. "Get them before they escape around the sides of the rake."

I saw three or four striped fish darting about in front of

me and I lurched back, flinging the pole into the water. It knifed into the surf and struck the sandy bottom. I pulled it out shaking my head, realizing this wasn't going to be as easy as Teuila made it look.

"Try again," she said. "You'll get it. But you have to act fast, before they escape."

I reared back and thrust the spear into the water a few more times, and on my third attempt it stopped half way underwater, shaking rapidly.

"Grab the stick!" Te' yelled. "Don't let it get away!"

The fish was twisting in a frenzy with the stick running through it, and I grabbed the pole as it slapped on top of the water, then lifted it above the surface to show my prized catch to Teuila.

"Not quite as big as yours," I said. "But not bad for a first time, what do you think?"

"You did great, Jade," Te' said, beaming at me. "Tomorrow, we'll build a retaining wall to funnel them toward us more easily. Then we'll have no trouble catching all the fish we can eat. Let's take a break to enjoy our catch."

As Teuila and I waded toward the shore, I looked around the lagoon and smiled. I knew I'd finally found my slice of paradise.

12

Teuila cleaned and filleted the fish we'd caught then we sat on the beach and enjoyed some fresh sushi marinated in pineapple juice and coconut cream. While we ate, she asked me about my life in the United States and I learned more about her culture on the island of Anuta. The more I listened to her, the more I began to envy her stress-free life in this tropical paradise. With each passing day, I was becoming less dependent on my Western comforts. For the first time in years, I didn't miss having my phone next to me.

When we finished eating, she examined our wounds and decided to keep the bandages on for one more day to let them fully heal. But there was no longer any need for me to wear my bra, and I happily threw it into the pit, symbolizing my liberation from the binds of Western civilization.

"So what's on our agenda for today?" I asked, bouncing up and down like a giddy schoolgirl. "Swimming in the crystalline waters of the lagoon and lounging on the beach?"

Te' ran her eyes over my pale breasts and smiled.

"As much as I'd like to rest and relax, I'm afraid we've got a fair amount of work to do. We don't know how long it will take for your friends to return. I want to build a more secure place for us to sleep, one that's better hidden from the lagoon and any foot patrols.

"Besides," she said, noticing the burn lines around my chest. "I think you need to be careful about getting too much sun too quickly. It's going to take a few more days for you to get a proper Anutian tan."

"Yes," I said. "Especially since I left all my sunscreen in my purse at your village. What kind of shelter did you have in mind?"

"One higher off the ground, in the trees. It might take us a couple of days to finish it. The most important material will be twine to hold the support beams in place. And that takes a bit of time to produce. But two people can do it twice as fast. Let me show you how to make organic rope."

Te' led me a few hundred feet into the forest until we came upon a clump of short, spiky bushes.

"This is the pandanus plant," she said. "Our tribe normally makes ties using bark, but the fewer trees we have to strip the better in case someone comes snooping around. The leaves of this plant are very fibrous and will be a good substitute."

"You can hold up a *house* with just a few leaves?" I said, bending the skinny stalks in my hand.

"With the right braiding, yes. Plant cellulose is an incredibly strong material, especially when it's properly twined."

She snapped one of the leaves off near the base, then ran her fingernail along its length to separate the fibers. She pulled a few of the stringy strands apart and lay them in her hand.

"Now they look even flimsier than before," I said,

shaking my head. "How can those skinny fibers hold much of *anything* together?"

"For such an enlightened culture," Te' smiled, "you Americans sure lead a sheltered existence. Watch what happens when we combine the strands and weave them together."

Teuila bunched the strands together in her palm and folded them into a long U-shape, then she bent one end down, forming a small loop at the joined end. As she pinched the loop with the fingers of her left hand, she twisted the horizontal band of strands away from her with her other hand while using her middle finger to lift the end pointing down and pulling it toward her, wrapping the two shoots around one another. She repeated this process for a minute or two, until she'd formed a six-inch-long line of interlaced strands that looked just like a braided rope.

"That's pretty cool," I said, nodding at how quickly she'd fashioned a rope out of natural materials. "But that doesn't even look long enough to tie around my wrist. What do you do if we need to make a longer rope?"

"It's simple to join extra pieces together," she said. "Watch carefully."

Te' gathered another bunch of leaf strands and folded them in half, pinching them tightly together at the fold. Then she inserted the V-end of the folded shoots into the open end of the braided strands and repeated the wrapping sequence, twisting the two ends of the joined strands away from her while simultaneously pulling the other two loose ends toward her. Within seconds, the loose ends of the first set of strands disappeared into the lengthening braid until there were only the short ends of the new set of strands remaining at the end of the rope.

"Holy crap," I said, shaking my head at how easy it was to

create any length of rope using just plant leaves. "But how *strong* is it? And how firmly connected are the two joined pieces?"

"Why don't you see for yourself?" Te' said, handing me the waxy twine. "Try to pull it apart."

I grasped the braid on each end and yanked it as hard as I could in opposite directions. Still not believing that a plant leaf could be so sturdy, I lifted my leg and wrapped the twine over my knee and pulled as hard as I could on each side. Still skeptical of its strength, I lifted it in front of me and bent it up and down a few times. When it began to splinter and crack, I looked up at Teuila triumphantly.

"Hold on, girl," she said, taking the leaf rope out of my hands.

"If you bend anything like that long enough, just about anything will break—even steel. But we're not going to use it that way. We're going to bend it around large poles and tie it in a fixed position. You saw how it's almost impossible to break with fixed tension. That's all we care about at this point. We're going to use it to *hold* things, not as a swing!"

"Okay," I sighed. "You've convinced me. How much of this stuff do we need to build our tree house?"

"A lot. A few hundred pieces of cord a couple of feet long should do it. If we separate the tasks and work together, it shouldn't take too long. Would you rather harvest the strands or braid them together?"

I held Te's bandaged hand and peered at the swelling around her finger.

"Which task will be easier on your hand? It looks like you still need a bit more rehabilitation time than me."

"The less twisting and bending, the better," she nodded, pinching her finger tenderly near the knuckle. "How about if I collect the leaves while you weave them together to start?"

"Sounds like a deal."

Teuila demonstrated one more time how to properly twist and join the shoots, then I sat down on a broken tree stump while she began to tear and separate the leaves. After a half hour or so, I'd assembled a decent pile of arms-length twine, and I shook my wrists trying to relieve the muscle cramps in my hands.

"That's a pretty impressive length of cordage," she said. "I think we're about halfway there. Would you like to switch positions for a while to rest your aching fingers?"

"If you think you're up for it," I nodded. "I'm not used to doing this amount of physical labor with my hands. I better pause for a while before I get repetitive stress syndrome."

"Repetitive *what*—?" Te' asked with a puzzled expression.

"It's another frailty of our Western culture. A lot of people sit around hammering away at computers all day long and develop sore wrists and hands. Something tells me this is not an affliction known to native Anutians."

"I've never seen anything like that," Te' said, shaking her head. "We tend to do most things around here in measured doses. There's plenty enough work to keep everybody busy doing different things at any one time. Between fishing, planting, cooking, swimming, and dancing, we keep our bodies fairly limber."

"I noticed," I said, watching Te's lean legs flexing as she stooped down to cut another bunch of leaves from the base of the plant. "I wouldn't mind switching positions for a while if you're up for it. I'd like to learn how to do everything your culture does. You never know when I might be stranded on another deserted island."

13

Te' and I worked for another hour or so splitting and weaving the leaves until we had an impressive pile of shiny green twine.

"That's a lot of rope," I said, wiping my brow with my forearm. "What do we do now?"

"Now for the *fun* part," she smiled. "We begin building our house in the clouds. Grab a pile of rope and let's see if we can find a suitable location."

As we began walking deeper into the forest, Teuila swiveled her head from side to side, scanning the thicket of trees.

"What are we looking for exactly?" I asked.

"Ideally, a tree that's not too far from the lagoon, but still out of sight from the beach. One with high, sturdy branches and a thick canopy to provide cover from the elements and any search parties. We can build the rest."

While we continued foraging through the forest, my mind wandered to the story of The Swiss Family Robinson, who built such a beautiful and intricate treehouse on their deserted island. But something Teuila mentioned bothered me.

"If we're going to be out of sight from the beach, how will my charter boat crew know where to look for me when they return?"

"I have an idea about that," Te' said. "The trick will be to build a marker that they can find, but my father won't so easily see. We'll focus on that tomorrow. Our priority today is to build a safe hiding place."

I glanced around the forest and noticed a tall mushroom-shaped tree standing in a clearing a few hundred feet away. It had a thick golden trunk and long stringy vines hanging down from its domed canopy. Broad horizontal branches radiated out in every direction about fifteen feet off the ground.

"How about that tree?" I said, pointing to the unusual specimen. "It looks pretty sturdy and well camouflaged."

Teuila turned in the direction of the tree and nodded when she caught sight of it.

"That's a banyan tree," she said. "It's perfect. It's even got a built-in elevator."

"If you're referring to those vines hanging down from the branches, that's not exactly what I'd call an *elevator*."

"Yes, but they're a lot less obvious than a ladder. If my father comes around, nothing will look out of place. He won't have any reason to believe we're hiding in the trees."

Te' walked up to the tree and grabbed one of the hanging vines, pulling herself up hand over hand until she reached the bottom of a branch. Then she grabbed the limb and flung her body upward in one quick motion, placing her feet on the branch and standing up.

"*Damn*, girl," I said, shaking my head at how nimble she

was. "You make that look like Tarzan. You really do know your way around this jungle, don't you?"

"It's easy, once you get the hang of it," she said. "Now you try it."

I grabbed the vine with two hands, then wrapped my legs tightly around the cord and pushed up. It took me a minute to shimmy to the top, and when I reached the branch, I couldn't pull my body over it like Teuila had, so I flung one of my legs over the bough and awkwardly rolled myself on top.

"Not quite as elegant as your technique," I said, standing precariously on the limb, holding an adjacent vine for support.

"You'll get the hang of it soon enough," she said, brushing some loose debris off my bare breasts. "You just need to learn how to climb the vine with less rubbing. Otherwise, it won't just be the bottom of your *feet* that get scraped up."

I glanced above me and noticed some teardrop-shaped fruit dangling from the branches.

"Are those *figs*?" I said, widening my eyes in excitement.

"Yes," Te' nodded. "And they look nicely ripe. Have you ever tried one fresh off the tree?"

"If they're half as good as your fresh pineapple and mango, I can't wait."

Tequila picked one of the purple pods off a nearby branch then pinched the skin with her fingernails and separated it in half, placing it under my nose. The pulpy seeds glistened in the crimson-colored syrup of the berry.

"It smells heavenly," I said, closing my eyes as I savored the floral aroma. I cradled the dewy husk in my hands and bit into it softly.

"Mmm," I hummed. "This is almost as good as sex. Sweet, juicy, and succulent. Just like you."

Te' plucked another fig off the branch and bit it in half, squeezing the moist nectar over her hand.

"I see what you mean," she smiled. "This is definitely getting me in the mood. Let's hurry up and finish building our nest so we can have some more fun."

As I finished eating my fig, I looked up at the web of golden branches above us, marveling at how far the crown extended out in all directions.

"At least we've got pretty good protection from above. Will those leaves keep us dry when it rains?"

"Only during light showers. We'll have to build a thatch over our heads to channel heavier rainfalls away."

"What about *beneath* us?" I said, wobbling on the thin limb. "What will keep us from falling between the branches?"

"We'll have to put some additional support beams in place. We'll use the twine to hold them together. Come on, it's time to go gather some more supplies."

Teuila led me back into the brush and we hacked down a handful of ten-foot-long poles about three inches in diameter. We carried the poles back to the banyan tree where she tied three crossbeams between two overhanging branches about fifteen feet off the ground. Then she placed the longer poles over the crossbeams, creating a webbed floor in the shape of a fan spanning between the radiating branches. After she taught me how to wrap and tie the twine so that each connection was tight and secure, it only took us a little over an hour to secure the floor. When we were done, she stood on top of the latticework and held out her hand.

"What do you think?" she said, inviting me to join her on

our newly installed deck. "Does this look more comfortable than lying in a pit for the evening?"

I stepped gingerly onto the web of poles and flexed my knees to see if it would support my weight. The poles bent slightly, like a firm mattress.

Te' sat down on the web and smiled.

"Lie down beside me and see how comfortable it is."

I lowered my body onto the lattice, then lay on my back. The hard poles pressed into my flesh, especially where we'd lashed the ties around the connections.

"Not quite as comfortable as my mattress back home, but at least it's less lumpy than lying on the ground."

"We're not finished yet," Te' said. "We still haven't laid the carpet for our new home."

"*Carpet?*" I said, pinching my eyebrows imagining how the rough surface of our jerry-rigged deck could be converted into something as smooth and comfortable as the broadloomed floor of my house back home.

Teuila took my hand and we shimmied down a nearby vine, then she led me a little deeper into the forest where she hacked off some wide strips of bark from a mulberry tree. Then she climbed a coconut tree and passed down a handful of long palm fronds. When we returned to the banyan tree, we cut and lay the thick pieces of bark horizontally across the webbed floor until all the gaps between the poles were covered, then we sat down again.

"Better?" Te' asked.

"Definitely," I said, surprised at how similar her construction technique was to the conventional wood-frame houses I'd seen built in the Midwest. "It's still a bit hard though. Will we sleep on it like this?"

"There's one last step," she said, handing me one of the palm fronds. "Now we're going to make the carpet."

She began tearing the leaves into one-inch-wide strips, laying the strips on the floor in neat parallel lines. Then she placed another strip perpendicular across the leaves and deftly wove it over and under each of the underlying strands. With each successive strand, the leaves began to form a beautiful two-foot-square mat of interlaced leaves that looked as pretty as any placemat I'd find at Crate & Barrel or Target. When she finished, Te' lay the mat over the bark and asked me to sit on it. The soft leaves absorbed my weight and felt as soft as carpet.

"This feels almost as comfortable as my broadloom back home," I said, running my hands over the cushiony mat. "But it's much *prettier*. The two of us might be able to find a whole new vocation when we return to the United States. People would pay big bucks for this kind of natural fabric. What *else* can you use this stuff for?"

"We use the same weaving technique to make baskets, handbags, fishnets, all kinds of useful objects," Te' said.

I shook my head at the myriad uses of the island's natural resources.

"You guys really are self-sufficient on this little island, aren't you?"

Te' smiled at me as she thinned her eyes.

"Are you sure you want to go back to America?"

"Ask me in another week or two. I'm growing more fond of this lifestyle with each passing day."

"Help me weave some more mats then," Te' said, happy to see me beginning to enjoy the crafts of her tribe. "We need to cover the whole floor and add a few more layers for extra cushioning."

"Our very own wall-to-wall carpet," I nodded.

As the two of us continued weaving our natural-fiber mats, I looked up at Te' and smiled with a silly grin.

"What are you thinking?" she asked. "You look like a child who's just discovered her first pearl shell."

"I'm just so happy to be with you," I said. "All this nesting makes me realize there's nowhere else I'd rather be in the entire world."

14

After we finished building our carpet of plant leaves, Te' and I made love until we fell asleep exhausted under the warm canopy of our new home. The last thing I remembered before my lids fell heavily over my eyes was the sight of the luminescent figs gleaming like Christmas tree ornaments in the fading light of the setting sun. In the morning, we picked some more fruit from the branches above us and playfully rubbed the sticky pulp all over our naked bodies before going for a cleansing dip in the lagoon.

As I emerged from the surf gazing at Te's sexy tanned body, I could hardly believe my luck. Fate, or happenstance, had landed me in a tropical paradise with the woman of my dreams. We spent the next half hour spearing fish for breakfast, then she placed the catch in a small holding pen we'd built out of large rocks near the shore.

"No fresh sushi for us this morning?" I asked, wondering why she wasn't filleting the fish right away as she had yesterday.

"I thought this might be a good time to teach you the

next essential step in your survival skills. I need to teach you how to build a fire. You never know when you might need one. Besides, fresh fish tastes even better when it's grilled over an open flame."

"I was wondering when we were going to get around to that. But are you sure it's safe? I thought you wanted to keep a low profile in case your father came snooping around."

"There's an art to building a fire with a low smoke signature," Te' said. "Just as there is to building one with a *strong* smoke signal, which might come in handy later. Let me show you how to gather the necessary ingredients."

By now, the soles of my feet had fully healed and all the rubbing on the sandy beach and jungle floor had begun to form a thick, leathery second skin. I was surprised how comfortable it was to scamper across just about any surface without any external protection. More importantly, Teuila's cut had finally closed and she was able to remove her bandage and use her hand freely. Now the only items of clothing either one of us wore was my fading cargo shorts and her tapa-cloth dress, re-fashioned as a wraparound loincloth. It felt exhilarating to traipse about our corner of the forest completely topless, unconcerned about the judging eyes of our neighbors.

Te' led me back into the forest where we began collecting dead twigs of varying thickness. When we had a handful, we returned to the edge of the beach where she dumped the pile in our old sleeping pit.

"There are three things to keep in mind when building a fire you don't want anybody to see," she instructed. "The first is the *smell* of burning material. We have an onshore breeze today, so at least we're protected from people approaching from the sea. The second is the appearance of the *flame*, which is why we're building this fire in a pit protected from surrounding lines of sight.

"But the biggest danger is from the *smoke*, which can be detected from further distances. The trick is to use the driest and smallest materials, so the fire burns more efficiently and doesn't smother. But first, we have to get it started, and for that we need some special materials."

Teuila grasped the shank of her adze and began scraping the blade along the edge of one of the longer branches, producing thin curly strands of dried pulp. Then she picked up the pile of filaments and rubbed them between her hands, breaking them into finer, shorter pieces.

"They look a bit like the strands we used yesterday to make cords," I said.

"You could use this to make rope also," she nodded. "But since this material is drier and more combustible, we're going to use it as a fire starter. But now that you mention it, we're going to need another three-foot long length of string. Do you think you could do that while I prepare the other elements? This time we'll need the rope to be a little thinner, so use about half the amount of strands for each side as before."

"No problem," I smiled. "After all the rope we created yesterday, that technique is indelibly imprinted on my brain."

While I lifted one of the fronds lying in the pit and began separating it into thin strands, Teuila chopped the long branch she'd shaved earlier into a two-foot length then chopped a small indent into the side of the branch on each end. Then she picked up a shorter dead branch about one inch in diameter and sharpened one end to a sharp point while rubbing the other end against a nearby rock to create a rounded stub.

"That doesn't look like a very efficient spear," I said, twisting the doubled ends of my palm strands into a thin rope.

"We're not going to use this as a spear," she said. "We're going to use it as a *drill*."

"A drill?" I said, raising my eyebrows. "But it doesn't have any thread."

My mind suddenly flooded with images of Tom Hanks' character in the movie Cast Away blistering his palms while he rolled a dry stick in his hands trying to build a fire.

"And what are you going to use to *turn* it? I'd hate for you to damage those pretty hands again."

"Don't worry," Te' said, smiling at me. "My hands aren't even going to touch it. We're going to build a *bow* to create the necessary friction."

While I looked at her with a puzzled expression, she picked up two pieces of flat driftwood and carved a small notch in the center of each board. When I finished splicing the strands of the palm leaf into a three-inch length of braided string, she took the cord and tied each end around the notches in the stick, bending it to create a tight bow.

"This is going to help us build a fire?" I said, shaking my head wondering how she could use the bow to generate any kind of friction.

"Oh ye of little faith," Te' smiled. "Watch and learn, my apprentice."

She took the short beveled stick and placed it against the inside edge of the string then twisted it a hundred and eighty degrees, creating a tight loop around the shaft. Then she positioned the rounded end of the stick into the notch of the larger piece of driftwood and placed the smaller piece of driftwood over the pointed end. Then she angled the bow parallel to the ground and began swiping it forward and back. As if by magic, the beveled stick began rotating rapidly in the shallow hole in the driftwood.

"Holy cats—you weren't kidding!" I said, amazed at the ingenuity of the device. "That way is so much more efficient than the way Tom Hanks did it!"

"Tom who—"

"It's just another one of our crazy Western stories that I'm sure you'd find amusing." I noticed Te' was pressing firmly on the top piece of driftwood as she sawed the bow. "Is there anything I can do to help?"

"When you begin to see smoke, place the shavings around the twisting piece of wood. We'll need to act fast to ensure the heat ignites."

I watched with fascination as Te' jerked the bow forward and back until the lower end of the stick started turning black and small wafts of smoke began rising from the fulcrum.

"Now, Jade!" she panted. "It needs fuel!"

I bunched the dry shavings around the edge of the stick, watching the smoke grow thicker and denser. When tiny orange embers appeared under the shavings, Te' bent down and cupped her hands around the pile, blowing gently into the nest. Within seconds, it erupted into flames as she began piling small twigs onto the pile. Eager to not have all her hard work go to waste in the fledgling fire, I began to throw a bunch of larger twigs and leaves onto the pile, throwing up a large plume of gray smoke.

"Be careful," she said, pulling the material off the flame. "We don't want to smother it. A fire needs plenty of oxygen to burn efficiently. If it has more fuel than it can burn at any one time, it just creates more smoke. The key is to feed it only as much as it needs to keep burning at the desired intensity."

Within seconds, the smoke began to dissipate as the fire steadily grew while she fed it increasingly large twigs and logs. When the flames reached a height of six inches or so, Te' looked up at me and nodded.

"We're almost ready to begin cooking our fish. Can you gather ten or fifteen small rocks so we can build a cradle for the grill?"

"Absolutely," I said, my mouth already watering at the idea of our eating warm food for the first time in three days.

When I returned to the pit with a handful of rocks, Te' placed them in a two-foot-wide circle around the fire then held some long branches above the top of the flame, charring them a dark brown color.

"I think we've got everything we need now," she nodded. "If you bring me two of the larger fish from the pen, I can cut them up and begin grilling them."

I went to the holding pen and snared two fish with a spear and carried them back to Teuila. She placed each one on the large piece of driftwood, cutting off its head and slicing it under its belly, removing the entrails and pulling the flesh away from the spiny skeleton. Then she spaced the charred poles about two inches apart over the top of our fire pit and placed the fillets on top of the makeshift grill. As the flesh began to sizzle, she fed the fire with medium-sized twigs, keeping the top of the flame a few inches below the slats.

"You're a master at this outdoorsy stuff, aren't you?" I said, shaking my head at how seamlessly she'd learned to live off the land.

"You get pretty handy at doing these things when you've been doing it your whole life," she said, turning the fillets over with her bare fingers. "Tonight, it'll be your turn. But for now, let's enjoy our new catch."

As we ate the perfectly charred fillets with our bare hands, I oohed and ahhed at how delicious the fish tasted.

"Ok," I said. "Scrap that basket-weaving idea I suggested earlier. I think your real calling is in the *kitchen*. I think we should open your own authentic Polynesian restaurant when we get back to the States."

15

After we finished eating, Te' and I strolled hand-in-hand along the shore of the lagoon while I stopped periodically to pick up pretty shells strewn along the beach. I marveled at the magnitude and diversity of the beautiful specimens, sprinkled like gleaming jewels across the pink-colored sand. Displaying in all kinds of shapes and colors, I felt like a kid in a candy store as I picked up the fascinating objects and turned them over in my hands.

"I've been to a lot of beaches in my life," I remarked. "But nothing like this. I've never seen such a huge variety and quantity of seashells ever. This is truly a magical island."

"Maybe it's because there's no other islands for hundreds of miles around," Te' nodded. "Or maybe it's just because there's fewer tourists picking them up."

"Is *that* what I seem like to you?" I said, pinching my eyebrows in disappointment.

"Well," she said, squeezing my hand playfully, "I suppose you're still technically a tourist since you aren't officially *living* here. But if you keep learning all of my native island secrets, we'll have to make you an honorary citizen soon enough."

As I continued picking up and examining one beautiful shell after another, Teuila suddenly became silent as she gazed out to sea.

"What's it like on the other side of the ocean, Jade?" she asked. "Will I be like a fish out of water in America?"

I stopped and placed my hands over Te's shoulders as I gazed into her eyes.

"Not as long as you're with me. You speak near-perfect English, and you have an amazing array of practical skills. I can teach you everything else you need to thrive in my country, just like you're showing me here."

"Does that mean you want to stay with me?" she asked with a pained face. "I don't know what I'd do if I lost you again."

I pulled her close to me, feeling her heart beating against my chest. For the first time since my first college affair, I felt that she was the only one for me.

"I will never leave you, Teuila," I said, squeezing her arms. "I've never felt such strong feelings for anybody my whole life. You're the only one I want to be with—forever and ever."

As we held each other close, I peered down at the warm water washing over our feet. Bobbing on top of the surf I saw a skinny threaded shell, shaped like the head of a spear.

"Look at that," I said, pulling away for a moment. "This one almost looks like a unicorn horn."

"A *what*?" Te' said, furrowing her brow.

"It's another one of our silly Western fairy tales. But it also reminds me a bit of your ingenious little fire drill. I think I'd like to keep this one as a memento of my trip to your island."

Te' rolled it around in her palm and nodded as she peered up at me.

"Would you like me to attach it to a wrist bracelet made out of palm twine? That way you won't lose it."

"I'd like that very much," I said, kissing Te' gently. "My very own Anutian charm bracelet."

Suddenly, a larger swell washed over our feet and I peered down seeing a shiny green stone. It was about an inch and a half in diameter and shaped like a heart, glistening in the morning sun. I picked it up and examined it carefully, shaking my head in amazement. Under its emerald-green coating, I could see tiny specks of black embedded in the rock.

"I can't believe," I said, shaking my head. "I think this is a natural Jade stone. What are the odds we'd find it on a remote beach like this?"

Teuila picked up the stone and turned it around in her hand, rubbing it gently with her fingers.

"It's smooth and soft, just like you. What a perfect name for such a pretty stone. Do you mind if I keep this one to remind me of you?"

"Of course not, baby," I said, my eyes tearing up in a swell of emotions. "Do you know what this unusual shape means?"

"Is it from another one of your American fairy tales?"

"In a roundabout way," I chuckled. "It's a powerful symbol of love where I come from, symbolizing the shape of our hearts that beat strongly when we feel especially close to someone. And I can't think of a more perfect memento for you to take away from your native island, because that's exactly how I feel about you."

I paused, as I gazed gently into her eyes.

"I love you, Teuila."

"If that's what all this pounding in my chest is that I'm feeling right now, then I guess I'm in love with you too, Jade. I think the Gods are trying to tell us something."

As I looked at Te' with tears of joy streaming down my face, I noticed some movement at the edge of the cape a few hundred feet offshore. I narrowed my eyes trying to focus on the object, then my eyes flung wide open when I realized it was the bow of a canoe slicing through the water. I grabbed Te's hand and pulled her behind one of the dunes.

"What is it?" she said, recognizing the fear in my eyes.

"It's a canoe," I said, pointing in the direction of the craft. "I think your father is getting closer than we hoped."

Te' poked her head carefully above the dune and peered in the direction I'd pointed, then ducked her head back down, her chest puffing up and down in frantic bursts.

"Is it from your tribe?" I asked.

"It looks like it," she said. "If we stay hidden, hopefully they won't come ashore. We haven't left any visible signs of habitation nearby. They're probably just searching the boundary of the island to see if they can find any sign of us."

As we lay flat against the side of the dune, I heard the sound of rhythmic singing emanating from the lagoon, growing progressively louder, then it began to diminish. After another minute or so, Teuila lifted her head again.

"What are you doing?!" I said, grabbing her hand. "They might see you!"

"It sounds like they're almost past the lagoon," she said. "I just want to see who they sent out to look for me."

Te' peered over the top of the sand for a long moment as her eyes grew wider and wider, then she ducked down again into the pit.

"What is it?" I said. "You look like you've seen a ghost."

"It might as well have been," she said. "Those men weren't from my tribe. They must be from the tribe on the other side of the island. And they weren't singing. Those were *war chants*. I think they have something far more sinister on their mind."

16

"There's another tribe on this island?" I asked. "Why didn't you mention this before?"

"I didn't think it was important," Te' said. "It's a big island and they usually stick to themselves, so I didn't think we'd cross them. But they're venturing further afield than usual and coming from the direction of my village, which worries me."

"Have the two tribes never had contact before?"

"Many years ago, we all lived together in peaceful harmony. But when a power struggle erupted between the chief and my grandfather, my *tama matua* was killed in battle and the chief banished the other faction to the other side of the island. My father became the chief of our clan and built fortifications to keep the other tribe away. Since then, everybody's been content to mind their own business. At least until now."

"What makes you think they mean to threaten your village?"

"It's unusual for them to venture so far from their side of the island. Their normal fishing grounds are to the north, not the west. And they were wearing war paint. But it was what they were *chanting* that worries me the most."

"What were they saying?"

"Something about taking back their land and reunifying their clan. I think they intend to recapture the women and children and kill off all the men. This was probably an advance reconnaissance mission to scope out our village's defenses before sending in their full war party."

"Oh my God!" I said, widening my eyes in horror. "What do you intend to do?"

Teuila paused for a moment as her gaze darted from side to side in thought. Then she looked up at me and frowned.

"I don't think I have any other choice. I've got to warn my father of their intentions before my tribe gets slaughtered. I'd never forgive myself if I didn't do everything in my power to save them."

I peered into Te's brown eyes, considering the implications of her plan.

"But aren't you risking your *own* freedom if you go back? After you've already disobeyed his wishes, he'll never let you out of his sight a second time."

"I can sneak in under cover of darkness and warn my nona. We can trust her to protect our safety. She'll tell my father, then we can retreat back to our hiding place."

"While you worry about the safety of your family? Do you really think you'll be able to stay here while there's a battle raging on the other side of the island?"

Te' looked at me with a pained expression. I could tell she was torn between the loyalty to her family and her love for me. My stomach sank, realizing I was putting her in an impossible situation.

She paused for a long moment as she considered her predicament.

"There might be another way," she finally said. "If I sneak into the other tribe's camp, maybe I can gather information about their plan. If there's still enough time, my father might be able to set up a meeting to defuse the tension. If the other tribe realizes that we know about their plan, hopefully they'll be less likely to attack."

"That sounds almost as dangerous as your *first* idea," I said, shaking my head in dismay. "What can I do to help?"

"I don't think you should go anywhere near either village. Your blonde hair and white skin will stick out like a sore thumb and be that much easier to detect. The best thing you can do is hide out here and wait for me to return. Now that you've learned the essential survival skills, you should be fine on your own for a couple of days."

"Screw that!" I said, fearing for Te's safety. "I'm not letting you go there alone. What if you get caught? At the very least, I can be a lookout and send for help if you get captured. You mean far too much to me. I'm not taking any chances that we'll get separated again."

Te' peered into my eyes and sighed in resignation.

"Okay. You can come with me—but only if you promise to stay further back while I scope out the situation. There's no point in both of us getting captured.

"Besides," she said, scanning my bare breasts, "there's no telling what they'd want to do with you if they got their hands on you."

"It's a deal."

"Come on then," she said, grabbing my hand. "There's no time to lose. We need to be there when the scouting team returns to their village so I can hear their plans."

Teuila picked up her adze and led me through the jungle, staying a few hundred yards away from shore to keep out of sight from the canoe team. Every now and then, a thin break in the brush revealed the wide expanse of blue surrounding the island, and she stopped to earmark the position of the passing boat.

"Do you know your way to their village?" I asked after she paused for another moment.

"Not as easily from this side of the island," she said. "But I've spied on them before on some of my longer hikes from my village. As long as we keep following the canoe, they should lead us directly there."

"Assuming they're heading to *their* village and not yours," I said, wondering if the angry tribesmen were already planning to attack.

"It's not a large enough team to overtake our village, even with the element of surprise. I'm ninety-nine percent sure this was just a scouting mission in preparation for the main invasion."

"It's that other one percent I'm worried about," I said, peering at Te's primitive hatchet. "If it came to an armed conflict, how would you defend yourself? Shouldn't we have brought the fire bow with us just in case?"

"That wouldn't do much good against an army of hundreds. It's too small to function as a weapon. Besides," she smiled, "that's one skill I still haven't taught you."

I shook my head at how quickly everything had begun spiraling out of control

"And here I thought the people of Anuta were such a peace-loving tribe."

"We normally are," Teuila said. "But some men's egos are easily offended. It appears that this next generation of chiefs still have a bone to pick."

"I just hope it won't be *our* bones they're picking over in the end," I said, re-imagining scenes of cannibalism among the warring tribes.

17

Dusk was beginning to set in as we approached a flickering light near the edge of the forest. Teuila held up her hand and crouched low as she peered through the trees. The team of canoeists were pulling their vessel up onto a sandy beach framed by thatch-roofed huts similar to those in her own village. A gray-haired man wearing a grass skirt approached the boatmen, flanked by a group of other young tribesmen. They paused to confer briefly on the beach, then they walked up the path and sat around a large fire burning in the center of their square.

Te' turned around and handed me her stone adze and small filleting knife.

"You stay here," she said. "I'm going to try getting closer to see if I can make out what they're saying."

I looked at the basic implements, batting my eyes wondering how they could possibly serve me better than her.

"What do you expect me to do with these?"

"Nothing, hopefully," she smiled. "They'll just slow me down. But you might need them if I get caught."

"What? To tomahawk the bad guys and cut you free?"

"Don't even think about trying that," she said. "If I don't return within the next hour, can you find your way back to my village to warn my father?"

I paused, looking up at the darkening sky.

"Not at dark, that's for sure."

"It will be easier if you double back to our lagoon, then try to pick up the trail from there. Worst-case scenario, just stay close to the beach and follow the island around until you get to our village. It might take a little longer, but at least that way you won't get lost."

"You're making this sound increasingly ominous," I said, wrinkling my brow. "Please be careful, Te'. Don't go any closer than you have to."

"Don't worry, my love," she smiled. "I've done this many times before. I should be back before the sun disappears over the horizon."

Teuila kissed me gently, then crept into the woods in the direction of the village. As I watched her tip-toeing through the trees, I marveled at how quietly she was able to pass through the dense brush hardly making a sound.

That's my girl, I nodded, peering up at the whispering canopy. *Don't even let the snakes know you're there.*

After a few minutes, she passed out of sight, and I squinted through the thicket, focusing on the circle of tribesmen seated around the fire.

It's true, I thought, remembering what she'd said to me earlier. *Why is it always the men who need to mix things up and create conflict?* I closed my eyes and imagined Teuila and me back in our little treehouse, living a peaceful life in our isolated stretch of paradise. I was in no hurry returning to all the stress and noise of Western civilization.

I picked up her adze and ran my finger gently over the edge of its blade. It was heavier than I imagined, and surprisingly sharp. I studied the head and shape of the handle, admiring how her people had fashioned such an effective tool out of basic materials. The stone head had been filed down to a sharp edge, with the butt of the blade supported by the extended arm of the ninety-degree handle. Tight cords of woven bark wrapped around the shank, securing it tightly to the frame. As I held it up wondering if it could be wielded as a weapon if the need arose, a deep masculine chant suddenly arose from the direction of the fire.

I peered through the copse of trees and saw that the men had raised to a standing position as they danced in a circle around the fire, flexing their spears and chanting loudly, just as I'd seen Manaia and the other young warriors from Teuila's tribe demonstrate a few nights earlier.

Maybe they'll kill each other off and let the two of us live peacefully on our own, I thought, shaking my head at their belligerent behavior.

I squinted my eyes, glancing from side to side to see any sign of Teuila. For the first time in days, I wished I'd had my phone or watch to keep track of time. It seemed like an eternity since she'd snuck off in the direction of the camp.

Where are you? I cursed under my breath, fearing she'd been discovered.

Seconds later, I heard some branches rustling behind me and I ducked defensively behind a bush.

"Jade!" Teuila whispered as I poked my head up.

"Thank heavens you're okay," I said, pulling her tightly

against me. Her bare breasts were warmer than usual, toasted from the heat of the enormous fire in the village.

"I said I'd never leave you again," she said, kissing me sweetly on the lips.

I held her closely, feeling her heart beating against mine, then I pulled away and looked into her eyes.

"Did you hear anything?" Do you have any clearer sense about their plans for attacking your village?"

"Yes," she said, tightening her face in concern. "And it's even worse than I thought. They intend to attack two nights from now, during the next full moon. We haven't any time to lose. I have to get back to my village immediately to warn my father."

Teuila picked up the blades from the ground beside me and pulled me back through the forest in the opposite direction of the camp. As we scurried through the brush, I shook my head in dismay. I wasn't sure which posed the greater threat—her father, or this new tribe.

18

B y the time we wound our way through the dark tangle of jungle to the other side of the island, the first glimmer of morning light had begun to appear over her village lagoon. Teuila paused at the edge of the forest overlooking the main square and peered in the direction of her hut. Everything appeared to be quiet and still, save the occasional squeal of a seabird returning from the surf with its morning catch of fish.

I glanced at Te', shaking more out of fear than from the cool onshore breeze.

"So what's your plan?" I said. "Everyone still appears to be sleeping."

"I'm going to sneak up behind my hut and try to get the attention of my nona. I want you to stay here and keep a lookout. If you see any unusual activity, whistle softly twice in succession."

"Won't that attract the suspicion of the tribespeople?"

"Not if they're still asleep. Just try to sound like one of those seabirds."

"Fat chance of that," I said, realizing I still had much to learn about her island. "What should I do if you get caught?"

"Same thing we talked about earlier. It'll be safer for you to return to our lagoon until things quiet down. I'll steal away when I can and find you."

I shook my head and furrowed my brow at the fragility of her plan.

"You might not have enough time. The other tribe is going to attack in two days."

"Once my father finds out about their plans, I'll be the least of his concerns. He won't be able to spare any extra tribesmen to watch over me. It shouldn't be too hard to break away during all the distraction."

I placed my hands around Te's arms and stared into her eyes.

"Just tell me no matter what happens that you won't stay and fight. I don't know what I'd do if I lost you."

Teuila smiled at me as she cupped my face and kissed me gently. Then she pulled the heart-shaped stone we'd found on the beach out of a pouch in her loincloth and patted her chest with the palm of her hand to symbolize the beating of her heart.

"You'll always be with me, Jade. *Forever and ever.*"

I pulled her close to me and squeezed her tightly against my chest.

"Please be careful."

Te' nodded, then crept quietly around the perimeter of the camp toward the chief's hut. As she disappeared behind the cabins, I glanced toward the beach and noticed Manaia stowing something in one of the village's outrigger canoes. It seemed odd that he'd be up alone at this early hour and I peered back toward Teuila, unsure if she'd seen him. For a moment, I pursed my lips preparing to send a warning signal. But he seemed unaware of her presence and I decided it was best not to risk any further distraction.

When I looked back in Manaia's direction, I noticed a flickering light emanating from inside the hull, as smoke began to rise above the gunwales.

He's setting fire to their outrigger canoe! I realized, pinching my eyebrows in confusion. *Why would he be doing that?*

Teuila had told me how important the village's few outrigger canoes were to their tribe and how long it took them to hollow them out from the thick trunks of the island's breadfruit trees. If they needed them as their sole method of navigation around the island and for deep sea fishing, what purpose would he have in destroying them?

Then it suddenly dawned on me. The timing of his act of sabotage was too coincidental. He must be a *spy* for the other tribe! By virtue of his status as Teuila's chosen mate, he'd have unique access to her father and his plans for protecting the village. He must have been offered some kind of preferential treatment by the other tribe for him to take such drastic action.

I turned back in Teuila's direction just as she slipped behind the rear of her family's hut. If I gave the warning signal now, she mightn't hear me and just attract the attention of Manaia. As I swiveled my head frantically back and forth between the two scenes at opposite ends of the village square, I heard some rustling coming from the chief's cabin. A few moments later, Te's grandmother appeared at the front entrance. She slowly swiped the door covering aside and tiptoed down the front steps toward the back of the cabin.

Te' pressed her finger to her lips when she saw her nona, and two women retreated further up the path away from their hut. I could see the two of them talking quietly at the edge of the forest, then her grandmother began gesticulating wildly with her hands, obviously upset about what Teuila had told her. When I turned back in the direction of the beach, I noticed two more canoes had been set aflame and there was no sign of Manaia.

I wasn't sure if he had escaped into the bush to rejoin his comrades, or if he'd retreated to his cabin to maintain the guise that the other tribe had sabotaged their canoes. Either way, Teuila needed to be warned so she could notify her grandmother of the betrayal within their ranks. I pursed my lips and strained to whistle as loudly as I dared.

It took longer than I hoped to attract Teuila's attention, and by the time she finally looked in my direction, the flap of her hut's front door swung open as her father stood in the entrance, peering from side to side. From her position many yards away from her family's hut, she was unaware that her father had been roused. I wanted to scream out loud to her and tell her to run, but by now many of the villagers had begun to stream out of their huts, attracted by the unusual smell of burning wood.

When the chief caught sight of the burning canoes, he hollered something in his native tongue and a swarm of tribesmen converged on the beach trying to put out the flames with baskets of seawater. But it was too little, too late. By the time they were finally extinguished and the gray smoke stopped pouring out of the hulls, all three of the village's outrigger canoes had been cut in half by the charred ruins of the fire.

When I looked back toward Teuila's hut, I was horrified to see that Manaia had found her and was holding her arms tightly behind her back as her father stormed back up the path in their direction. When he confronted his daughter, they hollered at each other for a few moments as Te' struggled helplessly against Manaia's hold. Her younger sisters and brothers began streaming out of the hut, and the chief muttered something to Manaia, motioning for him to take Teuila inside.

When they disappeared behind the door curtain, the chief castigated nona for helping his daughter then yelled to the tribesmen returning from the beach, pointing into the woods in my direction.

"*Saili latou!*" he shouted, as the angry warriors spread out into the jungle.

19

As the tribesmen darted toward me, my mind raced trying to devise an escape plan. All I could think about was Teuila's dream where her father tied me to a stake and burned me alive after he found us. It seemed like an extreme punishment for two lovers following their hearts, but from the crazed look in his eyes, I couldn't rule anything out right now. And with her jealous boyfriend demonstrating increasingly suspicious behavior, I'd have one more enemy wanting me out of the picture.

With the warriors fanning out in every direction, I knew running wasn't an option. I'd quickly be overtaken by their superior speed and familiarity with the terrain. And climbing another tree was out of the question. With so many eyes probing for the white girl, I'd stick out like a polar bear in the dark jungle. My biggest liability was my light skin and hair color. I needed to find a way to blend into the landscape—fast.

Picking up the stone adze Teuila had left behind, I hacked away at the ground, exposing the dark volcanic topsoil. I clawed at it with my fingertips and rubbed it all over my blonde hair and upper body, then shrunk behind a leafy bush as low to the ground as possible. Within seconds, I heard footsteps approaching my position with the sound of sticks beating the bushes.

Lying as still as possible not even daring to breathe, I closed my eyes praying that my clumsy camouflage job would keep me hidden for a few moments longer. The slapping sounds grew louder and louder until it seemed as if one of the searchers was standing right over top of me. Suddenly, something struck the ground next to me and I opened my eyes to see the sharp point of a stone-tipped spear plunging into the bush.

Jesus! I thought, realizing how serious these tribesmen were in apprehending their prey. My mind began to spin with all the possibilities. *Was it really me they were after? Had Teuila's father asked for me to be returned dead or alive? Maybe they thought I was the one who'd set fire to the canoes? Or were they looking for the saboteurs from the other tribe? Had Teuila even had a chance to tell her father about their plans to attack the village?*

While the tribesman continued jabbing his spear into the bush, I watched his dusty feet dancing over the ground not far from the gash I'd made with the adze. From my perspective inches away, it looked like an obvious mark inflicted by a recent intruder. As I lay on the ground with the sharp tool digging into my stomach, I wished I'd had the presence of mind to cover the fresh soil with some leaves.

But just as the tribesman stopped spearing the bush and I thought I was in the clear, I noticed some unusual movement sliding along the ground out of the corner of my eye. It was another three-foot-long snake winding through the brush! All the beating of the bushes in the surrounding area had scared it from its roost, and it was moving directly toward me. And this time, I knew that if it bit me, I couldn't count on Teuila and Nona to nurse me back to health.

As it slithered up over my arm toward my shoulder, I lay deathly still, holding my breath. At least I was aware of its presence this time. If I could just keep from flinching, maybe it would think I was another dead branch on the ground and leave me alone. I watched its forked tongue flickering in and out of its mouth like a divining rod. When it got to within inches of my face, I closed my eyes and prayed it didn't view me as a threat.

Why would it want to bite me? I thought. *I'm too big for it to eat, and I'm not threatening it in any way.* I remembered my father telling me on family excursions into the cottage country of northern Wisconsin that rattlesnakes were threatened by the vibrations of the earth in their vicinity. *As long as I remain still, it should leave me alone.*

As the snake paused next to my ear, I clenched my neck muscles unconsciously, expecting it to strike. But after a few seconds that felt like an eternity, it continued winding its body over my back and down the side of my torso, until it slithered off into the brush. The moment it left contact with my body, I gasped in a breath of fresh air as slowly as possible, trying not to make any sounds that might alert the nearby posse. I'd been so focused on the serpentine intruder, that I hadn't even realized the tribesman who'd been searching in my area had moved on. As I strained to listen for any nearby activity, I heard the sound of shouting receding into the distance, and I finally began to relax my muscles, pulling the sharp axe from underneath my body.

Now what? I thought, realizing I was still in a dangerous position, surrounded by a small army of warriors on the lookout for any suspicious movement. *How long should I stay concealed in my precarious hiding place? Should I wait a little longer to see what the chief intends to do with Teuila? Will he stop looking for me when he realizes he needs to start preparing for the impending attack?*

I had no way of knowing what kind of arrangements Te's father had made to prevent her escape. She'd told me to return to our lagoon and wait for her to come back, but what if she was tied up or had a twenty-four-hour guard? Maybe I could create some kind of distraction and cut her free.

I looked at my small stone adze and shook my head. With my luck, I'll get myself caught too and be no good for either one of us. I'll just have to spend the night here and see if I could find an opening at first light. I peered up at the bright moon, noticing that it was almost perfectly round.

Either way, we've got less than forty-eight hours before the crap hits the fan and someone's going to get hurt.

20

———

Teuila sat against the knobby walls of her hut with her hands tied behind her back, staring angrily into Manaia's eyes. He returned her gaze with equal intensity, as his lips curled into a menacing sneer. His eyes darted over her exposed body, taking particular interest in her loincloth wrapped tightly around her hips and waist.

She lifted her knees and pressed them against her chest, folding her arms around her legs. The idea of Manaia violating her made her sick to her stomach. Beyond the fact that she was madly in love with Jade, there'd always been something sinister about him that gave her the creeps.

"What do you *want* with me?" she asked in her native Samoan tongue.

"What makes you think I need anything from you right now?" he said.

"The way you're looking at me, for one thing. I've seen that look on men's faces before. I'm never going to let you touch me like that."

"We'll see about that," Manaia snickered, glancing back

down in the direction of her crotch. "We'll soon be married and you'll have no other choice. And this time you won't be able to run off with your girlfriend. We'll either find her soon or she'll perish in the jungle. Without you looking after her, she'll die of starvation or get bitten by another snake. Either way, there's no way you're going to escape this time."

Teuila huffed at Manaia, realizing he had no idea just how well equipped Jade was to survive in the jungle with her newfound skills. As long as she could evade the search dragnet currently underway, she should have no difficulty looking after herself until Te' could make her way back to their lagoon.

"You could *never* satisfy me like she does," Teuila taunted. "You men are only good for two things. Making war and making babies. And I have no interest in either of your plans. Her friends will soon come back for her and when they do, you'll never see me again."

"I wouldn't be so sure about that," Manaia said. "Her tiny crew will no match for our tribe of warriors. We'll be ready for them if they return, then remove any sign they'd ever been here."

Teuila thinned her eyes as she studied Manaia's face. Although her father was no fan of Western interlopers, she knew it wasn't his style to kill outside visitors. As chief of the village, Manaia and the others were still bound to follow his commands.

"My father would never do that," she said. "You know as well as he, that that would just invite more external aggression."

"Only if the outsiders have reason to suspect foul play. We have plenty of ways to conceal any evidence of visitation to our island. And besides, your father won't be chief for much longer. Soon, *I'll* be the one calling the shots."

Teuila squeezed her eyes together, unsure what he was alluding to. But right now, she had bigger concerns. She needed to warn her father of the impending attack and make sure Jade got to safety. She'd worry about Manaia later. The smirk on his face soon disappeared when the flap covering her hut's front door swung open and her father stormed into the hut.

"Where is she?!" he shouted angrily, standing over his daughter.

"Who?" Teuila said coyly.

"The Western woman! She can't have gotten far and you must know her hiding places. Tell me now!"

"I honestly don't know," Teuila said. "But you have more important matters to be concerned with right now. The *Tuange* tribe is planning to attack our village tomorrow night. You need to prepare our defenses or take preemptive action."

The chief stepped back, placing his fists on his hips.

"How do you know this?" he asked.

"I overheard their warriors discussing their plans when I followed one of their scouting missions back to their camp. They intend to steal the women and children and kill all of our men. You have to act quickly."

Manaia suddenly stood up and stepped toward me with an angry expression on his face.

"She's lying!" he said. "She's just making up this crazy story to distract our attention while she tries to escape again. We need to focus our manpower on making sure she doesn't get away. What she's been doing with that fair-skinned woman is an abomination."

"Shut up!" the chief said, turning toward Manaia, thrusting his hand against his chest. "*I* make the decisions around here, and we need to listen to Teuila's warning. I know what the *Tuange* is capable of, and we cannot take any chances at being ill-prepared."

Teuila's father swung back around and looked sternly into his daughter's eyes.

"Did they say if they planned to attack by land or sea? Were they the ones who burned our canoes?"

Teuila looked at her father with a confused expression and shook her head.

"They didn't mention anything about destroying our canoes. I got the impression they were going to wait for the full moon before they struck out for our camp. What do you intend to do, father?"

The chief stood for a long moment pondering his options, then motioned to Manaia.

"Gather the other tribesmen in the village square. We will need to organize our battle plans quickly. I will make sure my daughter doesn't escape again."

When Manaia rushed out of the hut, Te' struggled to stand. Her father placed his hand gently on her head and motioned for her to stay seated.

"I'm sorry to have to do this Teuila, but I can't afford to lose you again." He kneeled down and wrapped some thick strands of hibiscus twine around her binds then tied the new rope around a sturdy branch in the side wall. "You'll have to stay here until we sort this other matter out. And this time Nona won't be here to help you."

As her father stormed out of the hut and Te' struggled against the sharp twine digging into her wrists, a lone tear dribbled down the front of her cheek. It looked like regardless of the outcome of the looming war between the tribes, she'd soon be bound into the arms of one power-hungry man or another. She wiggled her leg and felt Jade's stone rubbing against her thigh.

Stay safe, my love, she thought. *Hopefully at least one of us can escape this madness.*

21

I woke up at first light the following morning with a growl in my stomach. It had been twenty-four hours since I'd eaten anything, and I swallowed hard realizing I was left to my own devices to feed myself. But I had more pressing immediate matters to attend to. I needed to see what had become of Teuila and find a way to extract the two of us safely from the village. We only had a little over thirty-six hours before all hell would break loose in the camp. The safest place for both of us would be as far away on the other side of the island as possible.

I slowly lifted myself up and parted the leaves of my bush, peering in the direction of the village. The square was busier than usual for this time of the morning, with sentries posted at opposite ends of the esplanade. A large group of tribesmen sat in the middle of the square sharpening stones, tying them carefully to the ends of long spears and arrows. Manaia paced around the circle, gesturing and barking orders like he was in command.

I glanced in the direction of Te's hut and saw that a guard was standing on all four sides of the structure. There was no sign of Nona or the chief, and from the stillness of the cabin, I assumed that Teuila and her family were still sleeping. After another twenty minutes or so, her father stepped through the front door and called to one of the tribesmen in the working group. He walked to the bottom of the steps, and as Nona and Teuila's siblings streamed out the front entrance, the chief motioned for them to follow the tribesman toward the lagoon. I took this to mean that Teuila had notified him of the other tribe's invasion plans and that he was taking no chances leaving the women or children unattended.

At least he's aware of the danger now and is taking necessary precautions, I nodded.

But where was Teuila? Why hadn't he sent her down to the lagoon with the rest of her family to attend to her morning ablutions? Was he going to leave her under armed guard in the hut all day, where she'd have to take care of her private affairs in a bowl?

I shook my head at the barbarity of his decision.

He's not taking any chances with her, I thought. *It's going to be next to impossible for her to escape with an armed guard surrounding her cabin and with her grandmother not allowed to go anywhere without an escort.*

I glanced toward Manaia again, wondering what he was up to. After destroying the village's only means of marine navigation, instead of slipping into the forest to join his comrades from the other clan, for some reason he'd chosen to stay behind and help his tribe prepare for the attack.

Was he going to join his tribe in battle, then turn on them at the last second? Or was he waiting for the right time to slip away and alert the other tribe that his village had been forewarned of their intentions?

I still wasn't sure if the chief intended to defend his

village against the attack or if he planned to take preemptive action. Either way, Manaia couldn't be trusted. I needed to find a way to warn Teuila and her father before it was too late. The other tribe looked to be at least twice as large as Teuila's. The only chance her group would have to prevail in the looming battle was to maintain the element of surprise. Manaia surely would have already informed the other side of her village's defenses and battle readiness. If he were to switch sides in the heat of the fight, that could easily turn the tide in favor of the other clan.

But how could I get close enough to her hut to send her a signal? Trying to whistle again was out of the question. After my last pitiful attempt to mimic the local wildlife drew her father's attention, I couldn't risk betraying my position again. My only chance was to leave some kind of message with her grandmother. But how could I draw her attention when she was being watched so closely?

I paused to rack my brain with every possibility. Then it suddenly dawned on me. Teuila had told me she'd studied many of the same subjects as me during the time missionaries visited the island. What if she could *read* English as well as she spoke it? If I could get her grandmother to pass her a note, I could warn her about Manaia's intentions and see if her father might relax his restrictions.

But how could I write her a message? I didn't have any writing material, and I'd left my phone in my bag in her hut when we escaped three days ago. I looked around for any object that might serve as a writing tablet, then I noticed a mulberry tree like the ones Te' said her tribe used to make their skirts and dresses. I knew that the inner layer of its bark was thin and pale. If I could strip a piece off, maybe I could carve a message into its pulp-like skin.

I got up on all fours and crawled toward the tree,

keeping a close eye on the village square to make sure nobody saw me. When I reached the tree, I used my small paring knife to cut a four-by-six-inch piece of bark off the trunk, then I lay it flat on the ground and found a small sharp stone nearby. Realizing I wouldn't have long before Nona and the rest of Te's family returned from the lagoon, I scrawled a rough message into the backside of the strip.

Watching close by. Manaia burned the canoes. Warn chief. Will wait for you at our lagoon.

I hid my adze and knife under the bush then stuffed the piece of bark in the back of my shorts and carefully circled around toward the lagoon. By now, I had a decent understanding of the layout of the village, and it didn't take long to wend my way through the woods near the trailhead to the bathing lagoon. When I got there, I saw Nona and the children walking single-file up the path with the tribesman urging them on from the rear.

I waited until she was close to my position, then I shook the branch of a low-lying tree to get her attention. She glanced in my direction and when she saw me hiding in the brush, she paused as I tossed the piece of bark toward her. The guard yelled something to her, then she kneeled on the ground and leaned over, pretending to be sick. The tribesman hurried past her with the rest of the children as he grimaced in her direction. Nona picked up the piece of bark and noticing the strange writing symbols on it, tucking it under her tapa dress. Then she nodded toward me and joined the rest of the group while the guard waited impatiently.

As the group continued marching up the path toward Teuila's hut, I doubled back to my previous hiding place and waited for her grandmother to deliver the news. When they returned to the hut, the chief stood on the front porch with his arms crossed and ordered them all back inside. A few minutes later, Nona stepped through the front door carrying a large wooden bowl and the chief jerked his head in the direction of the jungle. She tiptoed down the steps cradling the bowl carefully, then disappeared behind the hut and returned a few minutes later, sprinkling some loose sand inside the container.

So it's true, I grimaced in disgust. *The chief is making her do her business in a pail. At least it's affording her a little privacy to receive my message.*

Nona disappeared back inside the hut for a few minutes, then she stepped out and spoke quietly with the chief as she glanced nervously in Manaia's direction. The chief shook his head angrily, then he flipped open the door flap and stormed back into the cabin. I could hear he and Teuila talking in strained voices, then her father stepped out onto the porch and motioned for Manaia to join them in the hut. For the next minute or two, the sound of angry voices emanated from the building as the rest of the tribesmen turned and looked at one another in confusion.

Finally, the two men stepped out of the cabin and the chief said something to Manaia as he pointed toward the men working in the square. Manaia scurried to join them, but this time he sat quietly among them, joining them in their labor. Then the chief sat on his chair on the porch, motioning for the four guardsmen guarding his hut to maintain their positions.

That's it? I thought. *He's letting Manaia off scot-free? What about Teuila? Is he just going to leave her in there? Didn't she tell him about Manaia's treacherous behavior?* He must have convinced the chief that she was making it all up to drive a wedge between them in the hope of rejoining her white girlfriend.

It looks like we're on our own again babe, I sighed.

At least it looked like her father had temporarily demoted Manaia and was going to keep him in his sights for the time being. However he chose to address the coming assault, I couldn't help much sitting here in the crossfire between the two tribes. Besides, my stomach was getting increasingly noisy, telling me I had to get something to eat soon. I decided to head back to our private lagoon and try to catch some fish while I planned my next steps.

22

I t took me longer than expected to find my way back to our lagoon on the other side of the island. After getting lost a number of times, I had to retrace my steps more than once to get back on the trails that Te' had marked. By the time I saw the familiar shape of our crescent-shaped beach, the sun was almost setting over the horizon. I knew I wouldn't have long to catch some fish in the fading light, so I grabbed a spear from the treehouse and waded into the shallow waters of the lagoon.

Without Te' herding the fish toward me with the big rake, it was hit and miss trying to spear one, but I got lucky when a big grouper ambled nearby and I snared it on my second attempt. By this time, I was so hungry that I didn't bother trying to build a fire and instead tore open the flesh with my paring knife and dug into it like a grizzly bear eating fresh salmon.

When my stomach finally began to quiet down, I paused to consider my options. I knew that I could spend the night holed up in our treehouse in the hope that Teuila would find a way to steal away from her camp under the cover of darkness. But what if she couldn't escape? And what if her tribe lost the battle? What would the other tribe do to her? Even if her clan won, her father wouldn't be likely to let his guard down as long as I was on the lam.

I had to do something. I couldn't just wait here and pray that the odds rolled in our favor. There were far too many variables that could swing this in the wrong direction. With Manaia working to undermine his own tribe, there was no telling which way the battle could go. At the very least, I could keep an eye on the other tribe and send a warning to Nona and Teuila if I recognized any change in their plans.

I grabbed a few figs from our banyan tree to wash down the sushi, then I went for a quick swim in the lagoon to wash all the filth from my body. It felt refreshing to be clean again, and for a moment I thrust my hand down the front of my cargo shorts remembering the image of Teuila's naked body walking toward me in the lagoon. Then I quickly buried my leftovers and picked up my adze and pocket knife, following the trail toward the other tribe's camp.

With the light beginning to fade over the horizon, I struggled to remember the path Teuila had taken to make her way to the other village. After an hour or so, I became lost again and headed toward the shore to follow my way around the edge of the island. I knew the other tribe's camp was in a clockwise direction from our lagoon. If I just followed the shore, sooner or later it would lead me to their camp.

As I stumbled along the rocky shoreline, trying not to step on any sharp shells or sea urchins, I glanced up toward the sky. The moon was almost full, casting a bright glow over this side of the island. At least I could see what I was stepping on for the most part. The last thing I needed right now was to crack open the soles of my feet again. Whatever was going to go down over the next twenty-four hours, I knew I needed to remain fleet of foot and nimble.

As the moon continued rising over the shimmering sea, I began to hear the sound of men chanting in the distance. I peered to my right and saw the flicker of a fire burning in the distance. Recognizing I was getting close to the other tribe's camp, I stepped off the rocky shore and began to wind my way through the thick woods in the direction of the light. When I got to within a few hundred yards of the camp, I paused near a tree and crouched down low to get a closer look at the tribesmen assembled around the fire.

A large twig suddenly snapped underneath me, and I cursed under my breath for not being more careful where I stepped. Teuila had made it look so easy passing through the thick brush like a jungle cat, barely making a sound. Apparently, I still had a lot to learn about how to behave like a true Anutian.

When I looked back in the direction of the campfire, the number of tribesmen appeared to have thinned somewhat, and I wondered if they were sending out another reconnaissance mission to Teuila's side of the island. At least Manaia was nowhere to be seen, I thought. He's probably too afraid to try slipping away now that Teuila's father suspects him of foul play. He's undoubtedly waiting until the last moment to see which way the battle is going before he chooses which side to fight on. My lips curled into a sickening scowl imagining Te' wedded to that coward.

Suddenly, I heard some bushes rustling behind me and I twisted around to see what it was. Peering up in horror, I saw a band of painted warriors surrounding me with their spears raised over my head.

Damn, I thought, immediately recognizing I shouldn't

have been so eager to bathe in the lagoon. My white skin
and yellow hair were shining in the moonlight like a beacon
atop a lighthouse.

23

As the tribesmen shouted at me, angrily stabbing their spears in my direction, I shrunk back against the tree, fearing for my life. I had no idea what they would make of a half-naked white woman spying on their camp. From Teuila's description of the rift between the clans, I wasn't even sure they'd seen a Westerner before. One thing was for certain—they were in no mood for a peaceful welcoming committee.

One of the warriors noticed my adze lying on the ground and he picked it up, shouting something at me. I shook my head indicating I didn't understand what he was saying. He motioned to two of the other tribesmen and they lifted me up, finding my steel paring knife tucked under the waistband of my cargo shorts. He ran his fingers over the sharp blade and flinched when it drew blood.

Great, I thought. *Their first exposure to a white person, and the first thing they find are two weapons of mass destruction.*

The lead warrior said something to the other tribesmen, and they grabbed my arms, dragging me in the direction of the village. As I stumbled to catch my footing, I peered toward the large bonfire burning in the center of their camp. All my fears of being burned alive and eaten by cannibals were suddenly rekindled. I twisted and screamed for them to let me go, but the two men just tightened their grip on my arms until they were throbbing in pain.

As we approached the main camp, the tribesmen sitting around the fire turned toward me with puzzled expressions on their faces. Everyone was wearing grass skirts with war paint streaked across their naked upper bodies and faces. An older man with a beaded vest and elaborate headdress stood to greet the search party. The two tribesmen holding me marched me within three feet of the old man, then they forced me to kneel on the ground in front of him. I peered up at him and they shouted at me, pushing my head back down. I shook my head, unsure what they wanted me to do and the guards puckered their lips, tilting their heads in the direction of the man's feet.

This must have been some strange island ritual that I'd been spared at the other camp because of my infirm condition. I knew based on the superior elevation of Teuila's father's hut that the Anutians placed a high value on the height difference between individuals as a reflection of their relative power standing. It was obvious that this was the other tribe's chief and that as an unwelcome outsider I'd have to pay homage by submitting myself to his lowest level.

I looked at his dusty feet and leaned forward slightly as the two warriors nodded. Pinching my lips tightly together, I bent down and touched my mouth to the top of each of the chief's feet. He then motioned to the two tribesmen to lift me up, but when he saw that I stood three inches taller than him, he instructed them to push me back down onto my knees.

"*O ai oe?*" he said, grabbing my jaw and thrusting my face up to look at him.

"I'm sorry," I said feebly, "I don't speak your language. I'm from America."

"*Amerika?*" he asked, with a puzzled expression, peering at my faded cotton shorts and bare chest. "*Uana oe lava?*"

He seemed confused by my unusual appearance. I was pretty sure that if he'd ever seen a Western woman before, she would have been fully clothed.

The lead warrior stepped forward and presented my knife and adze to the chief, mentioning something as he motioned to me. The chief pinched his thumb gently over the end of the knife then turned the adze slowly around in his hands, noticing that it was well worn.

"*O fea na mua?*" he said, jutting it toward me with a furrowed brow.

He must have wondered what a naked Western woman was doing so close to his camp carrying one of their local tools. I wanted to tell him that I meant no harm and that Te' and I had noticed his tribesmen while bathing in our lagoon, but it was obvious that no one among the group spoke English.

"English?" I said, swinging my fingers from my lips, feigning a speaking motion. "Does anyone here speak *English*?"

The chief paused for a moment, then motioned to one of the tribesmen to fetch someone from one of the huts over-looking the square. A few minutes later, he returned with a native woman walking a few paces behind.

The chief mentioned something about *iglisi* to the woman, then he jerked his head in my direction.

"Do you speak English?" she said, looking at me.

"Yes, thank God," I sighed. "I mean you no harm. I'm here alone—"

The chief yelled something at the woman and she turned back to face me.

"What are you doing here?" the woman asked. "How did you get on this island?"

"I came on a chartered cruise from New Zealand. When our crew stopped to visit your island, I got lost and they left without me. I've been here alone for the last week or so."

The chief shook the adze angrily as he shouted at the woman.

"*O fea na mua!*" he repeated.

"Where did you get this axe?" the woman said. "It looks like one of ours."

I paused as I peered at the chief unsteadily. I wasn't sure how much I should disclose about my knowledge of the other tribe with so much tension brewing between the two clans.

"I met a native girl from the other side of the island," I said. "She taught me how to use it."

The woman said something to the chief, then he looked at me suspiciously, trying to discern my intentions.

"*Oe sakina mo latou?*" he said.

"Were you spying for them just now?" the woman translated.

"No," I lied. "I was returning from my camp when I got lost. I meant you no harm—"

The woman repeated what I said to the chief and he paused for a long moment, studying my face. I knew my story sounded improbable, but I hoped that he would find a naked Western woman carrying a stone axe as no threat.

He reached down and ran his hands over my head, rubbing his fingers through my hair. Then he leaned over and caressed my face, running his hands over my shoulders onto the front of my chest. Suddenly I felt less afraid and more embarrassed with so many male eyes ogling my naked figure. The chief cupped my breasts and squeezed them with his hands.

"*Fata masali!*" he shouted, peering around the campfire at his fellow tribesmen. They all laughed as he continued running his hands down my body. When he reached my shorts, he paused, feeling an unusual object under the cloth. He reached into my right pocket and pulled out the spiral unicorn shell that I'd found on the beach with Teuila.

"That's mine!", I shouted, reaching out to take it back.

The chief peered up at the translator, and when she told him what I'd said, he scoffed and threw the shell far to the other side of the sandy courtyard. Then he motioned for the two guards who'd carried me down the hill to tie me to a large pole standing in the middle of the square. As they lashed my hands tightly behind my back around the pole, I squirmed, screaming at the top of my lungs.

"What are you doing with me?" I cried. "I'm innocent! I don't have anything to do with the other tribe. Let me go!"

As the tribesmen reassembled around the fire laughing amongst themselves, the native woman paused, looking at me.

"Why are you doing this?" I said to the woman. "Can't you see I mean you no harm?"

"You're aligned with the other tribe. Our chief will keep you here until our grievance with them is settled. It's best that you don't resist. It will just make things more difficult for you."

As she walked back to her hut, I glanced at the group of tribesmen leering at my bare breasts. I had no idea what they intended to do with me, but the look on their faces gave me a sickening feeling in the pit of my stomach. I wasn't sure which would be a worse—being burned at the stake or getting raped by these savages.

As I dropped my head to my chest in resignation, I caught a glimmer of light reflecting off the sand near the edge of the fire pit. It was my unicorn shell.

"I'm sorry Te'," I said, realizing she'd have no way of finding me if she managed to get herself free. "I wanted to be with you. Hold close my love if I never see you again."

24

Teuila shifted her weight uncomfortably on the woven mat covering the floor of her hut. It had been twenty-four hours since she'd last seen Jade, and the crunchy sound of the leafy fibers reminded her of the first time they made love after building their treehouse. But the tight twine digging into her wrists quickly dispelled the pleasant memory as she began to focus on their current predicament.

She was pleased that Jade had evaded her father's dragnet and managed to pass word that she was returning to their lagoon, but there were still too many immediate threats that placed them both in danger. Compounding her anxiety, she didn't have any idea what her father's plans were for defending the village. If he decided to dig in and try to hold off the other tribe's attack, there was no way of knowing which way the battle would go. And if he chose to make a preemptive attack against their village, she'd be left here alone awaiting the outcome.

And with her father not believing Jade's story about Manaia's suspicious behavior, it was looking increasingly likely that either way, she'd be tied to him as long as she remained on the island. Even worse, Jade would be left to her own devices, with no way of protecting herself if Manaia mounted another concentrated search. Although she was capable of feeding herself and knew how to build a fire to stay warm, Jade didn't have Teuila's knowledge of the island or her ability to blend into the terrain. It was only a matter of time before either her father or Manaia would find her.

Jade's only chance now was for her sailing crew to return to the island and find her before the others did. But how would they even know she was still alive or where to search for her? Teuila wished she'd taken the time to help Jade build a marker atop a nearby hill to draw the attention of passing vessels. And what if she was bitten by another snake or stepped on a sea urchin? she thought. Jade didn't have Te's knowledge of the local plants to heal herself back to health.

Things were looking increasingly bleak for a happy reunion. Either Jade would be rescued by her Western friends or she'd be recaptured and sent home on the next cargo ship. Or worse, if she was found by Manaia. There was no telling what he might do to dispose of her in a more expedient manner. As Teuila's face contorted into an anguished grimace, the flap covering the hut's entrance swung open and the chief stepped into the hut.

Thank God! Te' sighed, thankful to finally have another chance to talk to her father.

"Father," she pleaded, twisting against the ropes tied behind her back. "Why are you treating me like this?"

"I'm sorry, Teuila," he said, squatting down into a cross-legged seating position in front of her. "But I can't trust you to not try running away again."

"So what if I did?" Teuila said. "What's so wrong about wanting to be with the person you love?"

Her father sighed as he shook his head dismissively.

"It isn't right for a woman to be with another woman that way. It's your duty to marry a man when you become of age and produce children to keep our community alive. Besides, running off alone breaks with our longstanding custom of aropa, where we've always shared everything communally."

"But I *love* her, father! I don't want to be with anyone else. If you loved me, you should want me to be happy."

The chief paused for a long moment as his face tightened with anguish.

"What makes you think this Western woman would be happy staying on this island with you anyway? She's ignorant of our customs and would soon begin longing for her material things. Eventually, she would just pollute our culture like the missionaries before her."

Teuila sighed, hesitant to tell her father of Jade and her plans to leave the island when her friends returned. She knew he'd never permit her to leave her family and the island. Beyond the insult to his personal authority, it would set a dangerous precedent for other members of the tribe. If she was allowed to go west, what would stop others from wanting to experience the temptations and luxuries of more developed societies? But she knew her father was right that Jade would likely soon miss her life on the other side of the ocean if they tried to stay.

"We've had a very happy couple of days living on our own on the other side of the island. Jade is beginning to appreciate the quiet comforts of our life on Anuta. But even if we did decide to leave, our community is strong enough to survive without me. Aren't you interested to know what life might be like outside our sheltered little island?"

The chief slammed his fists angrily on the floor of the hut, shaking the entire structure.

"You're already betrothed to Manaia!" he said. "No one is leaving this island. Our tribe has lived here in peace and harmony for hundreds of years. You are my daughter. I simply won't allow it."

Teuila gritted her teeth as she peered at her father impassively. She suspected his decision was based far more on his desire to protect his authority over his clan than a desire to maintain internal peace and harmony.

"What about this new aggression by the other clan? The peace is soon to be violently disrupted. How can you continue to protect us without outside help?"

"I have a plan for dealing with these renegades. We will attack them when they least expect it. I'm preparing a team to advance on their camp this evening. They will be too busy making their own battle preparations to anticipate our preemptive strike."

Teuila squinted at her father with a worried expression.

"Will Manaia be going with you?"

"Of course. He's one of our most powerful warriors."

"Do you really think you can trust him based on what Jade saw him doing earlier this morning?"

"That's just lies!" the chief said, flaring his nostrils. "She's making this up to drive a wedge between the two of you. Why would he do this?"

"Maybe he's been talking to the other tribe. If he knew of their invasion plans, this act of espionage would help protect him if they win. How can you be so sure he's not working for the other side?"

"I'm not completely sure he isn't," her father said. "Which

is why I'm keeping a close eye on him until we leave. We'll know soon enough if he's a traitor. In the heat of the battle, he'll have to choose sides. Either way, he won't have a chance to inform them that we're coming. We still have the advantage of surprise."

Teuila thought for a moment about her father's plan. There was something about the idea of including Manaia in the campaign that gave her pause.

"Let me come with you, father. I know the configuration of their camp and I'm skilled using a spear and arrow. You're going to need all the help you can muster against their superior numbers."

"This is a job for *tangata*," the chief said. "We can't afford to lose any more women from our tribe. Besides, I can't trust you to use this as another excuse to slip away."

Te' looked at her father with a painful expression.

"Father, you know I'd never abandon my tribe in a time of need such as this. Do you really think so little of me to believe that I would shrink from my duty to protect my village?"

The chief reached out his hands and cupped Teuila's face gently.

"I know you want to do what's best for your community. But leave this to us. I promise we will come back for you soon. I'm going to leave a small contingent behind to protect the village from any interlopers. When I return, we'll talk further about your plans. This will all be settled soon enough."

Te' twisted against the tight cords binding her hands.

"Can't you at least untie me while I'm under guard?"

"I'm sorry, Teuila. This is for your own safety. You're far too crafty. It's safer for you to remain in the village than be roaming over the island with so many dangerous elements on the prowl. We will celebrate our victory when we return with a wedding ceremony to join you and Manaia in marriage."

The chief kissed Teuila on her forehead then stood and exited the hut brusquely. Not long after, she heard the sound of warriors chanting war songs in the village courtyard. She peered through a gap in the wall of her cabin and noticed Manaia waving his spear menacingly as he glanced in her direction.

You might possess me soon, she thought, noticing the heart shape of Jade's stone pressing against her loincloth. *But you'll never own me.*

25

Teuila squinted through the narrow gap in the wall, watching the band of warriors dancing around the bonfire in the middle of the square. As their chanting progressively escalated in volume, her father exhorted them to be strong and brave. Whenever Manaia circled around and gazed in her direction, he seemed to have a crazed look in his eyes. Even though she knew he probably couldn't see her through the thin breaks in the wall, it seemed as though he was staring right at her. Then with a final flourish, the chief waved them forward, and they charged into the jungle.

Te' paused for a few moments, listening to the sound of silence, save the cackling of the fire outside her door. She couldn't see any further sign of movement through the slits in her cabin, and she wondered where the rest of the villagers were. She remembered that her father had said he would leave a few tribesmen behind to guard the village, but where was her nona and the rest of her family? Had they been sequestered to another hut to prevent her aiding

Teuila's escape again? It was strange to see her village so eerily silent at this early hour.

"Hello?" she called out, checking to see if anyone was guarding her hut. "Is anyone there? Who's protecting our village?"

"Be quiet, Teuila!" a young tribesman replied from outside the front entrance to her hut. "We don't know if there are spies watching us. We don't want to betray the location of the remaining villagers."

Okay, Te' nodded. *So I know I have at least one guard. It was clever of father to concentrate the women and children in a few huts. That way if the other tribe attacks, the remaining defenses can be concentrated on protecting a smaller perimeter. I guess I'm on my own until the war party returns.*

"Is there anyone else with you?" Teuila whispered to the guard outside her gate, fishing for more information. "How many warriors are left to protect our village?"

"There are five of us," the tribesman replied. "But don't get any ideas about trying to escape again. We have every side of your cabin under surveillance, so even if you were able to untie your binds, you'll be unable to leave the hut. Now shut up and let us focus on keeping an eye out for other threats."

Teuila paused to consider her options. She could stay holed up here and wait until the battle was decided before she made her next move. There'd be plenty of other opportunities to steal away into the jungle after things quieted down. Her father couldn't keep her tied up forever. She could try to escape and rejoin Jade in their private lagoon and fortify their defenses to avoid detection from any further searches. Or she could unite with her father in the attack on the other village and keep an eye on Manaia to make sure he didn't stab the chief in the back.

The more she thought about it, the less appetizing the idea of waiting it out seemed to be. There were far too many variables at play for her to risk the lives of her loved ones. Besides the threat to her father and the rest of his war party, there was her family and the rest of the villagers to think about. If her father lost the battle, there was no way of knowing how the victors would treat the remaining women and children. She knew they intended to kill all the men, but did that mean the young *boys* as well? And would the remaining women be simply absorbed into the new tribe, or would they be treated as sex slaves for the enjoyment of the conquering heroes?

And what of Jade? Even if she was able to find her way back to their lagoon and remain hidden, how could Teuila be sure she hadn't left a trail back to their hiding place? Te' knew how to use the riverbeds to hide her footprints, but Manaia and the other tribesmen were excellent trackers and would sooner or later pick up Jade's trail. Whether it was her tribe or the other clan that eventually found her, neither could be trusted to keep her safe and protected.

She knew that one way or the other, she'd have to find a way to escape to make sure that Jade was safe, then join her father and do whatever she could to ensure the success of their mission. But how could she escape from her hut if it was being monitored on all sides? It wouldn't be as simple as slipping out the back with the help of her nona. The first order of business was finding a way to break her bonds. She wouldn't be much use to anybody if she couldn't free her hands.

Te' wiggled her body along the floor until she found a sharp spur on one of the posts supporting the wall. Then she began rubbing the cords binding her hands as quietly as possible against the knob, trying to splinter the twine. She could hear the fiber pulling and tearing, but it took fifteen minutes before they finally snapped and freed her hands.

Now what? she thought, rubbing her aching wrists. *How am I going to get out of here with five people watching me?*

She peered through a gap in the far wall of her hut and noticed the diminishing reflection of the moon on the water, indicating it was moving higher in the night sky. Time was running out if she was going to have any chance to help her father. She already knew where the weak spots were in her hut, and for a brief moment she considered wedging out the back and making a dash into the woods. But if she got the timing wrong and was caught, she wouldn't have a second chance at her escape.

As she peered down at the leafy mats covering her floor, she reflected back to when she and Jade had built their own improvised house in the trees. She knew the floor of her hut was built the same way, with lashed poles supporting the foundation. If she could get underneath the webbed floor, the guards might not be able to see her while she planned her escape route. Teuila peered in the direction of the front door, watching the guard swiveling his head from side to side as he looked up and down the courtyard for any sign of suspicious movement. Then she pulled back a few of the leafy mats to inspect the floor more closely.

Each of the poles was spaced about an inch apart with tight binding connecting them every foot in length to keep them from separating. She would have to remove the ties from at least a dozen joists for a distance of three or four feet to have any chance at bending them enough to give her space to wiggle through. At least the ties were made from flat strips of inner bark instead of braided leaf strands, which would make it easier for her to dig her nails into the fiber to loosen the knots. But each of the ties were made in the form of a double constrictor knot, which made them all the more difficult to untie.

Te' cursed, realizing it was going to take longer than she hoped to disentangle the posts. She chided herself for not keeping the small paring knife for herself, but she realized Jade needed it as much as she did.

I guess we'll just have to do this the natural way, she thought.

For the next half hour, she painstakingly pinched and pulled each of the ties until they fell away to the floor of the pit six feet below the raised platform. Then she pulled two of the poles in opposite directions until the posts bunched together, leaving a narrow hole to squeeze through. Taking one last glance in the direction of the front door to make sure she wasn't being watched, she squeezed her legs and upper body through the hole, then dropped silently to the ground below, flexing her knees to absorb the impact.

Fortunately, the foundation of her hut was surrounded in leafy thatch similar to the kind coating the walls, so she had a modicum of cover concealing her from prying eyes. She crept to the back corner of her hut and parted the leaves carefully, peering out the crack. There were two guards standing at opposite sides of the hut keeping a close watch on the edge of the jungle for any suspicious movement. With a good twenty feet from the edge of her hut to the forest, there was a good chance she'd get tackled before she was able to reach the brush.

She'd have to create some kind of diversion to distract the guards, then slip over to the adjoining cabin from which she'd have a better chance to steal into the jungle. She looked around the base of her hut and found a large rock then picked it up and parted the curtain. She waited until both of the guards were looking in the opposite direction, then she threw the rock as far as she could straight into the opposite brush. The guards looked at one another, then one of them motioned for the other to check it out.

As the first guard stepped into the bush to investigate the disturbance, Te' pulled the leaves covering the side of her hut aside and sprinted across the lane, diving underneath the adjacent cabin. She waited a moment to catch her breath, then she parted the covering at the back of the new hut to see if the coast was clear. By this time, the other guard had returned to his position, shaking his head to indicate that it was likely just a bird rustling the leaves. From her new position, Te' could see that she was still too close to the guards to attempt a dash into the woods, so she crawled across the laneway separating the next two huts and took shelter one cabin further away.

But with each cabin further from the chief's signifying a lower status in the tribe, the floor of the third cabin was only a couple of feet off the ground, and she had to crawl on her elbows and knees to reach the furthest side away from the guards. As she rustled through the leaves, she could hear children's voices above her, so she knew this was one of the cabins that was being used to hide the remaining villagers.

But she didn't have any time to check on their wellbeing. She lifted the grass skirt at the far end of the cabin, then crawled out into the laneway, crouching low as she peered in the direction of the guards. She waited once again until they were looking in the opposite direction, then she prepared to sprint to the cover of the woods. Just as she was about to leap forward, she felt a hand touch her on the shoulder. Turning around fearing she'd been discovered by one of the guards, she was surprised to see the face of her grandmother peering through the slats in the wall, reaching out her arm toward Teuila.

Teuila squeezed her hand and Nona nodded silently toward her, blowing her a kiss with her other hand. No words needed to be spoken between the two women. They both knew where Teuila was going, and her grandmother simply wanted to wish her well. Te' looked up at Nona and lifted her finger to her lips, instructing her to keep the children quiet. Then she glanced in the direction of the tribesmen guarding her hut and leaped to the edge of the forest, disappearing quietly into the jungle.

26

Teuila knew she'd lost precious time fashioning her escape and that she'd be hard-pressed to catch up with her father. There was no time now to check up on Jade to make sure she was safe. She had to assume that she'd found her way back to the lagoon and that she would wait for Te' to return as she'd promised. There'd be plenty of time to attend to Jade later. Right now, her priority was to catch up with the war party and make sure Manaia didn't stab her father in the back.

The good news was that by now she was familiar with her way to the other tribe's camp and was able to cover the distance in half the time. Still, it took her almost three hours to traverse the island, and by the time she neared the other tribe's camp, the moon had risen almost directly overhead. As she neared their village, she heard the sound of tribesmen singing and chanting around a flickering light in the distance. Not wanting to set off any warnings in case her father was still preparing to attack, she found a point on top of a hill overlooking the village and peered around the woods trying to locate the position of the war party.

She couldn't see them on any of the high ground, but as she glanced down the slope, she saw the backs of warriors creeping through the jungle in a semi-circular formation, closing in on the tribesmen prancing around the fire. When she turned her head to make sure the other tribe was unaware of the encroaching invasion, her eyes suddenly flung open when she caught sight of a familiar blonde figure tied to a stake in the middle of the square.

It was Jade! How had she managed to get captured by the other tribe? And what were they planning to do with her?

Teuila could see logs and kindling spread around the base of the post she was tied to in the familiar shape of a fire starter.

Oh my God! Te' thought. *They're planning to burn her alive! Just as she'd feared in her wildest dreams!*

But as she watched her father's war party creep closer to the fire pit, she realized Jade was in grave danger of *another* threat, just as severe. Her position next to the band of targeted warriors placed her in the middle of the coming crossfire. Teuila had to get her out of there as quickly as possible. As she began sprinting down the hill in the direction of the camp, she heard the war party scream as they surged out of the woods, flinging arrows and spears in the direction of the tribesmen.

Hold on, my love, Te' thought as she crashed through the underbrush. *I'm coming for you!*

27

My legs trembled in fear as I watched the chanting tribesmen circling around the fire. I had no idea what they were saying, but judging from the brightly colored war paint adorning their faces and the intensity of their intonations, they must have been preparing for something big. But I knew their attack on Te's village wasn't due for another twenty-four hours. Was all this in preparation for the planned invasion, or were they getting worked up for something else?

I peered down toward my feet and got a sick feeling in my stomach. The twigs and logs assembled around the base of my stake looked threateningly similar to the type Teuila had used to start the fire in our lagoon.

Were they really going to burn me alive? Simply for stumbling onto their camp carrying a few small tools?

I'd always been reluctant to travel to third-world countries because I wanted to have the rule of law to protect me in case anything went wrong. But this was taking the abuse of human rights to an entirely new level. *What kind of barbarians would treat another human being in this way?*

At least they haven't raped me, I thought. *Yet.* Then I shuddered at another possibility. *Maybe they're planning to cook me in preparation for a special feast.* My charter captain had dismissed the notion of cannibalism being practiced in this region of the world, but Teuila hadn't explicitly denied it. Maybe these villagers looked at the odd stray Westerner who washed across their shores as a rare delicacy to be enjoyed in the same way we looked forward to the occasional roast turkey or rack of lamb.

I cursed at my stupidity for ever having strayed from the group hiking inland after we'd set ashore. But then I'd never have met Teuila, who was the most special person I'd ever known. I'd never have known a love as strong and pure as the kind I'd experienced in the short time we'd been together. There was something sweet and innocent about her, unvarnished and uncorrupted by Western civilization. The ironic thing was that we'd *both* stretched the boundaries of what we'd previously imagined possible by being thrown together in this unlikely place.

It was this clash of cultures that had brought me both the greatest joy in my life and the greatest despair. And now it was all about to end in the most horrifying way imaginable. Even worse, there'd be no way for Teuila to know what had become of me. She'd have to live the rest of her life thinking her lover had abandoned her without even saying goodbye after her friends returned to pick her up. There would literally not be a single human remain left of me for her to put the clues together. I closed my eyes and said a prayer, asking God to make the ending quick and to look after Teuila.

But just as I began my supplication, I heard the loud shouts of tribesmen approaching from the woods. I opened my eyes to see scores of painted warriors closing in on the men around the fire as they flung arrows and spears in their direction. The local group turned to face the attacking horde, hurling their own spears in self-defense. Within seconds, the attacking group had closed in on the surprised tribesmen, engaging in hand-to-hand combat with their makeshift axes and knives.

My eyes suddenly flung open when I recognized Teuila's father grappling with one of the tribesmen on the dusty ground. They rolled side-over-side a few times in the sand until Te's father gained the superior position. Then he raised his adze over his head and slammed it down, splitting the other man's skull in half.

Suddenly I heard the sound of another warrior's scream, and I looked up to see the crazed face of Manaia running toward me holding a flaming spear. Just as he reared back to fling the spike toward my helpless body, his face contorted in agony and he flopped to the ground with a large arrow sticking into his back. Standing a few feet behind him, Teuila stood wearing a lopsided grin. She nodded toward me, then she reached behind her back and grabbed a series of arrows from her quiver, felling the few remaining warriors still standing from the other tribe.

Within minutes, the battle was over as the warriors from the other clan lay sprawled on the ground around the fire with one or more stone objects embedded in their lifeless bodies. Te's father lifted himself off another dead tribesman, and after satisfying himself that the threat from the other side had been neutralized, he noticed Te' and approached her with an angry expression.

"*O lau o fae inerti?*" he shouted, acting surprised to see her.

"*Mea tau!*" she replied, holding her bow up and pointing toward the tribesmen she'd killed with her arrows.

The chief nodded in appreciation, then he recognized Manaia's figure lying on the ground and turned him over. Manaia groaned as he reached around toward the arrow still embedded in his back. Teuila's father said something to him, then turned him over on his stomach to inspect the wound. Then he grasped the shaft of the arrow and pulled it out of Manaia's shoulder and flung it onto the ground. He motioned to one of his men to bring him a tapa-cloth sling and Manaia sat up gingerly, placing his injured arm in the pouch. He glanced up at Teuila, pinching his eyebrows suspiciously, and she looked away from him disdainfully.

Te' strode up to my stake and began loosening the binds holding my hands behind the pole, but she paused when her father barked a command to her. She protested whatever he was saying, then he stormed toward me and pulled her hands away from the pole.

"What's going on?" I said, peering into Te's eyes. "What is he saying?"

"He wants to leave you tied up until he figures out what to do with you. He doesn't want to take any more chances that either one of us will run away."

"Oh Te'," I suddenly cried, overwhelmed to see her again. "I thought I'd lost you forever."

"Not as long as I live and breathe," Te' said, clasping the side of my face with her hands and kissing me firmly on my lips.

For now, at least, we were together again. But from the angry look on her father's face, I had no idea for how much longer it would last.

28

For the next fifteen minutes, the chief huddled with Teuila and Manaia as they gestured toward me in a heated discussion. Manaia seemed particularly agitated, pointing back and forth between me and Teuila like he was blaming us for the interclan rivalry. He walked over to where her father had discarded the arrow fired into his back and inspected it carefully, then he carried it back to the chief, shaking it angrily in Te's face. The chief muttered something to Teuila and she dropped to her knees in front of him, begging him to accept her version of the story.

Finally, he swept his hands in a dismissive motion and gestured to one of his guards to attend to me. The guard pulled a sharp adze from the side of his skirt and began walking toward me in a threatening manner. I could only assume from Te's anguished expression that her father had instructed him to kill me, and I closed my eyes, steeling myself for the worst.

At least it will be quick this time, I thought, tensing my body in anticipation of the final blow.

But instead, the guard circled around behind me and

began sawing at my ties until my hands were free. I looked up at Teuila, breathing a sigh of relief, but she just peered back at me sadly, shaking her head. The chief said something to the guard and he pulled my hands behind my back and retied them, then he connected a longer cord, which he wrapped around his hand. Te's father pointed to three more guards and motioned toward the remaining villagers cowering in their huts, then he lifted his hand and waved it in a circle, indicating that it was time for the rest of us to return to the village.

The tribesmen got in formation behind the chief and the guard who was bound to me pushed me in the back with the butt of his adze, instructing me to join the line. Te's father said something to Teuila, then she led the way back into the jungle with the rest of the troop following dutifully behind. As Manaia took up the rear position, I looked back at the sad faces of the women and children peering on from the entrance of their huts and wondered what would become of them. The whole scene reminded me of something out of a Vietnam War movie, with me taking the place of the captured soldier having to do a forced march back to the prison camp.

By the time our band returned to Te's village, the morning light was beginning to stream over the lagoon and the women and children raced out of their cabins, overjoyed to see that their side had won the battle. The men were exhausted from the night-long march, but Te's father pointed to the middle of the square, motioning for them to begin work on something. The guard who was tied to me escorted me to the location where the chief had pointed and forced me to sit down in the sand. Then the rest of the group disappeared into the woods as they began hacking down trees and branches of different sizes.

When they returned, they dug four deep holes in the sand on either side of me, then they placed a long stake in each pit, being careful to shore each one up so that it stood firm and steady. I watched dumbfounded as they began erecting a webbed scaffold all around me from the smaller branches, tying the posts tightly together with cross-ties of threaded bark. As they scurried up and over the structure like spiders, Te' reached out her arm and held my hand while the wall slowly rose between us.

"What's happening, Te?" I said, horrified they was caging me up like an animal.

"My father doesn't trust us to be together," she said. "He plans to keep you in this enclosure under close guard until either your friends return or the next cargo ship passes by our island. He doesn't want to take any more chances that either one of us will escape before then."

I glanced up at the lattice of poles rising above me and noticed they weren't building any kind of door into the structure.

"Don't you think this is a bit extreme?" I said. "How am I supposed to go to the washroom?"

Te' frowned sheepishly as she pointed toward the back corner of my cage.

"There's a small opening at the base of your enclosure through which we can pass a bucket and plates of food. I'll make sure you're kept as clean and well fed as possible until the ship arrives."

I reflected back on the image of Nona carrying a bowl in and out of her hut while Te' was being held in detention. At least there she had the advantage of covered walls to protect her modesty.

"They want me to do my business in plain sight of all the other villagers?" I said, hardly believing my ears. "Jesus, Te'—this is worse than a Turkish prison. At least there, you have a modicum of privacy."

Teuila squeezed my hand as she looked at me painfully.

"I'll talk to my father about placing a drape over your enclosure. I know it seems harsh, but he could have decided on a far worse course of action. As long as you're still alive, there's a chance we can find a way to be together."

I glanced behind Teuila and noticed Manaia conferring quietly with the chief as they watched us suspiciously.

"What about Manaia? Doesn't your father believe our story about him being a traitor?"

"Unfortunately not. He thinks Manaia comported himself bravely in battle and that his injury was further evidence he was fighting for our side."

I allowed a slight curl to form in the side of my mouth.

"So he doesn't know that you shot the arrow that injured him?"

"He has his suspicions, but there were a lot of arrows flying in every direction during the battle. My father is convinced that it came from one of the other tribesmen."

"And I suppose he also doesn't believe that Manaia was trying to kill me just before he was injured?"

"There were too many people running around, and he was busy fending off his own attackers. It's my word against his."

"And he believes *Manaia* over his own daughter?!"

"Unfortunately, he's already seen where my allegiance lies, which is with you. He has no reason to believe Manaia had any motive to betray his own tribe."

"So what happens now? What will become of you once your father gets rid of me?"

Teuila glanced down toward my feet as a tear dripped down her face onto the sand.

"He intends to marry me to Manaia tonight after everyone is rested, in celebration of our victory over the other tribe."

"Even though you've made it clear that you want nothing to do with him?" I said, shaking my head in dismay.

"It's no use. My father doesn't understand how two women can be in love the way we are. He insists on following the custom our tribe has practiced for hundreds of years. He expects Manaia and me to produce lots of babies and live happily ever after. He's convinced that once you're out of the picture, I'll regain my senses and settle in to a normal family life here in Anuta."

My face tightened into a painful expression as I peered into Te's eyes, realizing how hopeless our situation had suddenly become.

"Maybe he's right," I sighed. "Maybe I'm just pulling you away from what is natural and right. Maybe I'm just another Western intruder chipping away at your culture, leading you down a path of destruction and heartache, like the explorers did with the people of Easter Island."

"No Jade," Te' said, clasping my arms with both hands. "It's just the opposite. You've opened my eyes to the joy of true freedom and helped me recognize the opportunities outside my tiny sheltered island. It's my *father* who's been oppressing me and my people. I'm just expressing my free will and following my heart to be with the person I love."

"Oh Te'," I said, reaching between the poles and pulling her close to me as the last of the tribesmen stepped away from my completed cage. "I love you more than you'll ever know. I just don't see how—"

Seeing that my enclosure was now fully secured, Te's father stormed up the path and grabbed her arm, pulling her away from me.

"*Alu mai te ai!*" he shouted, glaring angrily at me.

As he dragged Teuila kicking and screaming back to their hut, Manaia locked eyes with me and sniggered a lopsided grin. I collapsed my body against the webbing of my enclosure and began sobbing, knowing I'd never have another chance to run away with my island girl.

29

———

After Teuila left, one of the tribesmen planted himself in front of my cage and stared at me impassively, while the rest of the village resumed their usual activities. Every now and then, some small children ran past my enclosure, pointing at me and giggling. Most of the men had retired to their huts to get some rest, but the women were busy moving about the courtyard with handfuls of provisions, preparing for the big celebration later this evening. I glanced in the direction of Te's hut and noticed her grandmother shaving some taro root on the porch, trying not to look at me. Her hut was surrounded on each side by a guardsman holding a spear. Inside, the dwelling was quiet and still, and I wondered if Teuila had been tied up again to prevent her escape.

So that's how it's going to be, I thought. *The chief is going out of his way to keep the two of us separated and confined.*

I looked at my guard and shook my head. I felt more exposed than ever with my bare breasts on display for everyone to see, like some kind of hooker standing behind the glass in Amsterdam's Red-Light District. I crossed my arms over my chest and sat down in the sand, and before long fell asleep from sheer exhaustion.

A few hours later I woke to the sound of chatter and noticed some tribesmen erecting a long trellis-shaped structure in the middle of the square. A band of women followed closely behind, decorating the lattice with garlands of flowers. My skin felt hot from the overhead sun beating down through the open bars of my cage, and I pressed my fingers against my flesh realizing I was beginning to burn. I picked up some sand from the base of my pit and tried to coat my body with it, but it just fell off my skin like dry confetti. Peering up at the sun, I estimated it was around noon, and I wondered how these people expected a pale white woman to survive all day long, exposed in the tropical sun. It had also been almost thirty-six hours since I'd had anything to eat, and I clutched my stomach from the gnawing feeling in my gut.

Te's father disappeared into their hut, then a few minutes later he came out carrying a few bowls and some folded objects. He spoke with Nona and pointed in my direction. Nona placed some items in one of the bowls, then she took the materials from his hand and began walking toward me. Upon reaching my cage, she bent down and slid one of the bowls through the narrow hole at the bottom of the enclosure.

When I saw that it was filled with fresh fruit and vegetables, I picked it up and gobbled it down like I'd never seen food before. Nona nodded toward me and passed a hollowed-out coconut shell filled with water through the bars and I emptied it in three gulps. As my stomach began to settle, I looked at her and smiled, placing my palms together and bowing to thank her for her act of kindness. Even though I knew she couldn't speak

English, I hoped she'd be able to share some news about Te'.

"How is Teuila?" I said, pointing toward her shack. I swiveled my wrists together in a shackled motion. "Is she tied up?"

"*Eh le lelei,*" she nodded, recognizing her granddaughter's name. Then she placed her hands over her heart and spread her palms in my direction. "*Na te misia oe.*"

I choked up understanding her meaning and swallowed hard, knowing that Te' was thinking of me. I looked at the other materials she'd placed on the ground outside my cage and recognized some woven mats similar to the ones Te' and I had made to line the floor of our treehouse.

"Are those for me?" I asked, motioning to the mats.

She nodded then said something to my guard, and he unfurled the mats and threw them over the top of my cage like two long table runners, one on each side. Nona straightened the leafy curtains until they extended all the way down to the base of my enclosure, then she slid one of the drapes aside so we could see each other.

"*Mai le Teuila,*" she said, pointing to my newly created canopy.

I returned Nona's gesture, placing my hands over my chest and extending them toward her in gratitude.

"Thank you."

Then she picked up the last object on the ground, which looked like a small hollowed out stump. She placed it between her feet and half-squatted over it, nodding and pointing to me. I nodded back, understanding her meaning, then she pushed it through the little hole at the bottom of my cage and rearranged my curtains so that I was almost completely covered.

I placed my hand over my heart again and blew her a

kiss, then she walked slowly back in the direction of Te's hut. As I watched her walk away, I reached out and rubbed a piece of the leafy matting between my fingers. The strands were still bright green and pliant, like they'd been recently harvested, and the weaving pattern was exactly the same as the one Teuila had shown me days earlier. I leaned my body forward and closed my eyes, breathing in the fresh scent of the pandanus leaves. For a moment, I imagined I could smell Te's scent on them too, and I wondered if she'd had a hand in making them. Either way, I was grateful she'd sent them to me as I sat down in the dark shade of my little hut and finished off the rest of the food Nona had brought me.

At least they're not going to let me starve out here, I thought, grimacing at the makeshift toilet bowl. *Looking after my other personal needs is going to be a whole other nightmare.* But the shade from my leafy umbrella was already starting to cool the inside of my cage, and I soon fell asleep dreaming of making love to Teuila on the floor of our treehouse.

I awoke many hours later to the sound of singing and chanting coming from the courtyard. I pulled my curtain aside and saw the villagers seated in long rows on opposite sides of the floral-decorated trellis leading toward a giant bonfire burning in the middle of the square. The flames reflected off the face of Te's father sitting atop his chieftain's chair, flanked by his children sitting squat-legged on the ground beside him. As the tribesmen hopped and skipped around the fire, the women and children sang gleefully at the top of their lungs.

Standing stoically in front of the chief with his arms folded over his chest, Manaia peered expectantly down the path in the direction of the trellis. He wore a long grass skirt like the other tribesmen, but unlike the rest of the bare-breasted warriors, he wore a beaded vest festooned with brightly colored sea shells and an elaborate feathered head-dress. Posing like a flamboyant peacock, he looked ridiculously overdressed for the occasion. But with his exaggerated sense of self-importance, it seemed to fit his personality perfectly. I fingered the unicorn-shaped shell that Teuila had reclaimed from the sand of the other village, wishing it were a dagger I could throw at him instead.

But Teuila and her grandmother were still nowhere to be seen. As the singing and dancing slowly increased in pitch and volume, I recognized some movement on the front porch of their cabin. Nona swept the front door mat aside, then Te' stepped out onto the portico looking like an angel from heaven. Wearing a white tapa dress dyed in a pretty floral motif, she wore a long wreath made of frangipani and jasmine around her neck and a crown of orchids atop her head. Her face shimmered in the moonlight, with a green-ish-yellow dusting of turmeric powder and flower pollen coating her upper eyelids. I gasped at her beauty as her grandmother took her arm and escorted her down the front steps of their cabin.

As they strode toward the trellis marking the entrance to the reception, Te' glanced in my direction and I slunk back toward the rear of my cage. For some reason, I didn't want her to see me watching her as she prepared to get married. Whether it was from my own sense of dread at losing her once and for all or from some misguided feeling of not wanting to ruin her big day, I lurked in the shadows, closing my eyes listening to the chanting of the wedding partici-pants. But after another minute or so, I couldn't resist the urge to see her one last time, and I pushed my screen aside to see the two of them walking under the trellis toward the fire in the direction of Manaia, who was grinning in front of her father like a Cheshire Cat.

So this is the way they do it here in Anuta, I thought, nodding at the similarities between the Polynesian wedding and those in the West. *The groom waits patiently by the altar, while his bride-to-be tantalizes him by slowly walking up the aisle as their loved ones eagerly look on. The only difference was that the mother of the bride, or in this case her grandmother, gives the girl away. Typical male-dominated culture, where the patriarch sits on his high horse as he watches his daughter given away.*

The two women walked together through the floral-covered trellis, then Nona disengaged and joined the rest of her family as Teuila approached the raging fire.

How appropriate, I thought, watching the shadows flickering over Manaia's smug face. *From the mother's arms into the fire.*

I half-expected Teuila to leap into the flames and self-immolate to escape the clutches of her treacherous groom. But then I realized that her father still had me to use as leverage to force her to go through with the ceremony. It was probably no accident that he'd placed me in the middle of the courtyard for everyone to see as a reminder of his absolute power over the rest of the village. He'd probably threatened to kill or torture me if Teuila didn't abide by his wishes and marry Manaia.

When Teuila got to within arm's reach of Manaia, he reached out and took her hand then they both turned around to face the chief as a hush fell over the crowd. Her father muttered a few words to them both, then he threw up his hands in exaltation, shouting to the rest of the crowd. Suddenly, the women and children poured off their benches, as they joined the tribesmen in excited dancing around the fire. At first, Te' seemed reluctant to join the festivities, but Manaia grabbed her hand and swung her boisterously around the fire with all the other celebrants. Whenever she came back around facing in my direction, I could see her glancing at my enclosure, but I squinted through the narrow breaks in the leaves, remaining hidden. I was too ashamed for her to see me trapped like a rat in my dark and dirty cage.

For the next two hours, the entire village sang and danced and feasted in celebration of Teuila and Manaia's union. After a while, I could no longer bear witness to the tragedy of the spectacle, and I curled up on the sandy floor of my cage, holding my hands over my ears trying to block out the sound of all the merrymaking. Eventually, the cacophony began to subside and I pulled my curtain aside, noticing the villagers slowly returning to their huts. Manaia and Teuila sat with her siblings finishing the plate of food laid out on the buffet, then her father said something to them, nodding toward one of the huts next to his own.

As the bride and groom stood up and began walking hand-in-hand across the sandy courtyard, I couldn't help noticing the bounce in Manaia's step as Te' dragged her feet through the sand. He seemed determined to consummate their marriage as quickly as possible, pulling her by the arm as she lagged two feet behind. They stopped at the base of the steps leading up to the cabin next to her own. Like the chief's, it was elevated much higher above the ground, signifying their newly elevated status.

Unbelievable, I thought, shaking my head in disgust. *All he has to do is marry the chief's daughter to elevate his status to second-in-command within the tribe. It's only a matter of time before he finds a way to take over command of the entire island.*

Manaia pulled Teuila reluctantly up the steps of their cabin, and just before they disappeared inside, she turned and glanced in my direction. My heart leaped out of my chest, and for a moment I considered flinging my drape aside and crying out to her to tell her how much I loved her. But Manaia yanked her inside and within minutes I heard the sound of pounding floorboards as he had his way with his new bride.

I closed my eyes and prayed forgiveness for ever having planted the seed of doubt in Te's mind. If it hadn't been for me, she'd never have known any other way than that of a man. I'd ruined it for her for the rest of her life. Teuila would forever pine for my tender touch as long as she remained on this far-flung island. I collapsed to the ground and sobbed, watching the tiny rivulets of tears roll away over the sand.

30

The next morning, I woke early with a sick feeling in my stomach. I'd dreamt Te' and I were swimming in our lagoon when a sea monster breached the surface and pulled her underwater. I reached out trying to grab her arm, but all I could do was watch the sad look on her face as she faded away into the depths. Realizing how accurately my dream mirrored the reality of our situation, I leaned over and retched into my wooden toilet basin.

Looking for a bit of light to pull me out of my depression, I pulled the blind across on the south side of my crate and noticed another guard sleeping in the sand a few feet away. I checked the other side and saw that my original guard was lying still on the sand with his eyes closed. The sun was starting to peer over the horizon at the far end of the lagoon, and with the village still quiet, I began to think about an escape plan. If I could just find a way to break out of my pen and sneak past the guards, I could return to our hiding spot and wait for Teuila to rejoin me. Once she knew I was free and safe, there would be nothing holding her back from escaping on her own.

I surveyed the construction of my cage and pushed it firmly on the side to see if it would give. But the heavy posts embedded deep in the sand at the four corners meant it wouldn't be as simple as toppling the tightly strung structure onto its side. I kneeled down and burrowed under the base of the enclosure with my hands, but the soft sand quickly backfilled into the hole. The guards were beginning to get restless, and I didn't want to take any chance at the digging sound pulling them out of their slumber. My only chance would be trying to untie the straps holding the poles together and slip out before they woke.

As I dug my nails into the cords and began loosening the ties, I kept a close eye on the guard on the south side of my crate. There were fewer huts between me and the forest on this side, plus I could use the shelter of the lagoon if necessary to hide underwater as Teuila and I had done at the swimming hole. But my finger slipped while untying one of the knots, and I squeaked in pain as it twisted against the wooden pole. The guard suddenly stirred and when he saw what I was trying to do, he leaped up and yelled at me, flinging a handful of sand in my direction. Some of the grains landed in my eyes, and I staggered back against the other side of my cage as they welled up in pain.

I batted my eyelids as tears streaming down my face, and within a minute or so I was able to recover my sight. The drapes had been pulled to the side of my enclosure, and the two guards barked at me as they thrust their spears in my direction. I slunk back onto the sand at the base of my pit while the guard on the lagoon side refastened the loosened ties, pulling them extra tight with double knots.

A few minutes later, Teuila emerged from the front of her hut and she began walking toward me carrying a few items. I smiled at her as I wiped the tears from my face, throwing a handful of sand into my bucket to cover up the smell of my vomit. As she approached my enclosure, she noticed the redness in my eyes and furrowed her brow with a worried expression.

"Good morning, Jade," she said, trying to cheer me up. "I brought you some fresh food and other provisions. How have you been holding up?"

"As well as can be expected under the circumstances," I smiled weakly.

Te' pulled the shades back across my enclosure, glaring at the guards for not giving me enough privacy. For a moment, I considered telling her about my failed escape attempt, but I figured it would just inflame their already raw emotions even further.

"Are you finding the drapes I made for you are keeping things a bit cooler in here?"

"Yes, thank you," I said, happy to hear that at least she wasn't being tied up in her hut.

"I thought you might like a bit more protection against the sun and the prying eyes of the villagers," she said, handing me a folded white cloth through the bars.

I unfolded the garment and smiled, seeing that it was a dress similar to the one she'd replaced from the previous night's wedding ceremony. I pulled it over my head then pressed against the bars, desperate to feel her touch. She reached out and squeezed my hands as we pressed our foreheads together.

"Te'," I moaned. "I've been thinking of you so much. I watched the ceremony last night, then I heard you with Manaia in the hut—"

"Don't pay any mind to that," she said, pulling back to peer into my eyes. "He may possess my body, but my heart will always belong to you. We just have to wait a few more days until things quiet down, then we can find a way to escape this god-forsaken place."

"What about the two guards?" I said, noticing the tribesmen still scowling at me. "How can we hope to escape with them watching me twenty-four hours a day?"

I glanced in the direction of her hut, fearful that Manaia or her father would see her with me.

"And what about Manaia? What if he finds us? I have a feeling that he and your father won't be as lenient if they were to catch us again."

"Let *me* worry about them," Te' said. "I know how to keep Manaia distracted. He's sleeping right now. We'll have plenty of opportunities soon enough. They'll never find us on the other side of the island."

I shook my head, remembering how easy it had been for the other tribesmen to catch me.

"Have you seen any sign of my sailing crew? The sooner we get off this island, the better. I think I've had quite enough of the tropics for a little while."

"There's been no sign of them. But my father says a cargo ship is due to pass by any day now. We won't have long before you're sent away."

She lifted a bowl full of figs and sliced pineapple, and I closed my eyes, breathing in the heavenly aroma.

"Are you hungry?"

I nodded, and she pushed the bowl through the hole in the bottom of my crate.

"This reminds me of our first day in the lagoon," I said, lifting the sweet fruit to my parched lips. "I remember waking up to the fresh scent of these hanging above our treehouse after we made love that night."

"It's all I can think about too," Te' said, squeezing my

hands so tightly they began to turn red. "It's the only thing that keeps me going."

I looked at Teuila with sad eyes and frowned.

"I'm sorry, Te'. I should never have come to this island. If you had never met me, you'd never have known anything different—"

"I'd still know what it feels like to be abused by a man," she said. "If it weren't for you, I'd have never known what it feels like to be truly loved by someone."

"Oh Te'," I cried, thrusting my body against the front of my crate and throwing my arms around her. "I don't want to lose you. I can't imagine my life without—"

Suddenly, the flap covering Teuila's hut swung open and Manaia turned to face us, glaring angrily in our direction. He quickly descended the steps and began running in our direction, and Teuila turned around and began running toward the woods. But he already had a healthy head start, and he quickly closed the distance, tackling her in the sand. Then he picked her up and threw her kicking and screaming over his shoulder, snickering at me as he strutted back up the steps of his hut. Soon after, Te's father emerged from his cabin and nonchalantly sat down on his rocking chair.

Teuila wasn't kidding about the men on this island, I thought.

As the thumping sound resumed in Te's hut, the chief leaned back in his chair and began to rock it slowly, nodding to my guards to keep a close watch over me.

31

For the rest of the day, I didn't hear from Teuila and wondered if Manaia had tied her up in their cabin to prevent her from communicating with me. Fortunately, Nona kept me well fed and hydrated, emptying my toilet bowl every few hours to keep my enclosure tolerable. I had plenty of time to ponder my situation, and the more I thought about it, the more hopeless I realized our predicament had become.

It would be nearly impossible to escape from my cage under twenty-four-hour guard. And with Manaia keeping a short leash on Teuila, she'd be hard-pressed to find a way to slip away before the cargo ship arrived. Almost as worrisome, I wondered why my sailing crew hadn't yet returned for me. It had been almost two weeks since they'd abandoned the island, and I couldn't understand why they'd left in such a hurry.

Had they run into members of the other tribe who threatened to harm them if they didn't leave immediately? Had they aborted the search once they realized how large the island was and how much ground they'd have to cover to search all of it? Had Teuila's father convinced them that I was likely dead after they'd stopped by the village? Or were they going to get reinforcements to search for me more thoroughly?

Either way, I didn't have much time before this was going to be out of my hands. There'd be very little I could do to salvage my relationship with Teuila once I left the island. It wasn't like I could come back with a team of mercenaries and forcibly abduct her. For all intents and purposes, Anuta was a sovereign nation and I'd be flaunting the rules of maritime law by interfering with their right to privacy.

And once I left, what chance would Teuila have escaping the island on her own? Even if she managed to evade Manaia's clutches, he and the rest of the tribe would hunt her down until they found her. With hundreds of miles of open ocean surrounding Anuta, there'd be no way for her to navigate to friendlier waters using one of the few remaining outrigger canoes.

The isolated beauty of the island was both a blessing and a curse. It was the tropical paradise where I'd found the love of my life, but it was also a refuge from which few could ever hope to escape. What right did I have invading their personal space, thinking I could steal away their most important daughter? Anutians had lived for centuries in peace and tranquility until I arrived. Teuila wouldn't even have known what it felt like to experience lesbian love if I hadn't contaminated their culture with my promiscuous Western values. I was acting like the typical arrogant American, thinking I could impose my superior Western mores on their backcountry civilization.

I slept fitfully that night, tossing and turning while trying to reconcile my selfish desire to hold on to Teuila with my knowledge that I had no right to intervene in the tribe's personal affairs. I awoke the next morning to the smell of fresh sea breeze wafting under the curtains of my hut. I pulled the blinds aside and watched the sun gleaming off the pristine waters of the lagoon as children ran playfully across the sand. Their mothers and grandmothers looked on from the porches of their huts as they prepared another healthy breakfast of fresh fish and locally harvested vegetables. On the beach, a team of young tribesman were busy chipping away at the trunk of a felled breadfruit tree, hollowing out a new canoe.

I smiled at the bucolic scene, realizing I had no right trying to interfere in their tranquil life. Suddenly, I noticed movement in the direction of Te's hut and I saw her grandmother walking toward me with a heightened sense of urgency. She had a strange look on her face, like she knew something foreboding was coming. When she approached my cage, she glanced at the guards nervously as she passed me a handful of fruit. A curl of bark fell to the sand and she gestured for me to pick it up. I leaned down and unfolded the husk, noticing some writing had been etched onto the inner skin.

"*Mai Teuila,*" she said, placing her hands over mine. Then she turned around and hurried back to her hut past the imposing figure of Manaia, standing on his veranda with his arms crossed.

I unfurled the parchment and read the message scrawled into the pulp.

Cargo ship on the horizon. Will be here within two hours. Manaia is not letting me leave the hut. If I don't see you before you leave, find your way back to our treehouse. I'll meet you there as soon as I can. Thinking of you always, love Teuila.

As I stood reading the message, my heart beat a hundred

miles an hour. I wanted to scream out across the courtyard to tell Te' I loved her and would never forget what we'd shared. But that would betray the vow that I'd made not to meddle any further in their affairs. But I couldn't just leave without saying goodbye. I had to let her know what she meant to me. I ran my fingers through the sand at the base of my enclosure and found a small stone. Then I peeled off the top layer of the bark and placed Te's message in my pocket. I sat down in the sand and began to scratch a new message on the parchment.

Dearest Teuila,

I'll never forget the delicate love and tenderness we shared during my short stay on your island. I'll carry the precious memories with me as long as I live. But I don't want you to pine for me after I leave. Your people share this wonderful culture of aropa, and in time I believe you will grow to appreciate the peaceful comforts of your community. I'll always be with you in mind and spirit.

I signed the note with a heart symbol and the letter J scrawled inside. Then I pulled the curtain aside on the side facing the chief's cabin, noticing Nona weaving quietly on the front porch. I feigned a cough and she looked up in my direction. I looked around to make sure I wasn't being watched, then I motioned with my hands for her to come back toward me. I knew this would be my last chance to leave a message with Teuila before the ship arrived.

She placed some fruit in a bowl and carried it back to me, and when she slid it through the slot in my cage, I dropped the husk in the pot and looked up at her. She paused for a moment, and I nodded as she slid the scroll under her dress.

"For Teuila," I said, pointing to her hut. "Thank you for all your kindness."

I steepled my palms in front of my chest and smiled, bowing in gratitude.

At least Teuila won't be entirely on her own once I leave, I thought. *She'll still have the love of her siblings and grandmother to keep her spirits buoyed.*

As Nona walked back toward her hut, I closed my blinds and sat down on the sand of my crate and began to sob uncontrollably.

32

———

For the next couple of hours, the village square was a bustle of activity as the children pointed excitedly toward the horizon and the men began bundling up piles of shark fins they'd caught on their recent fishing expeditions. A foghorn sounded from the direction of the lagoon, and my guards began dismantling my crate. Soon after, the bow of a large cargo ship glided into view beyond the cape. As a small skiff jetted toward the beach, Te's father and grandmother emerged from their cabin. Nona was carrying my handbag, and as they began walking toward me, I realized this was to be my final sendoff from the island.

I glanced in the direction of Te's hut and noticed that it was eerily still. It was obvious that Manaia was keeping her from me, and I suddenly began hyperventilating at the thought of not seeing her again. It seemed unimaginably cruel of him and Teuila's father to deny us the opportunity to say one last goodbye.

When the guards pulled the last of the ties away from my crate, they each grabbed one of my arms as Nona handed me my handbag. It was obvious that Te's father wasn't going to take any chances that I wouldn't be getting on the boat. I looked inside my handbag and noticed that everything was just as I had left it. It felt strange and surreal to see all the usual trappings of my old life lying in the bottom of the bag. There was my bikini, a bottle of sunscreen, my smartphone, and of all things—a business card, which must have fallen out of one of my travel guides as a bookmark. It was hard to imagine returning so abruptly to my privileged life on the mainland.

The guards escorted me down the courtyard toward the beach, and as I began stepping into the boat, I turned around one last time, hoping to catch sight of Teuila. Suddenly, she leaped out the front door of her hut with Manaia in hot pursuit and began running down the path toward me. This time she was the one with a head start, and it only took a few seconds before she traversed the full length of the courtyard and flung her arms around me. As Manaia pulled up behind her breathing heavily, the chief held up his hand and nodded, indicating he was going to permit us a few moments to say our goodbyes.

"Jade," Teuila cried with tears streaming down her face. "I got your message, but I don't understand. Don't you love me anymore?"

I pulled away and cupped Te's face gently in my hands.

"Of course I do, baby. I'll never stop loving you. I just wanted you to see the inevitability of our situation. You belong here on Anuta." I glanced at her grandmother and her siblings looking on from the porch of their hut. "You're surrounded by people that love you."

"But what about *you*?!" she said. "I thought you said you were starting to like it here? We could hide away on the other side of the island."

"If we stayed here, we'd eventually be hunted down. And your father will never let you leave this island."

I choked up, fighting to say the words.

"It's time to move on. I'm sure that once I'm gone, everything will quiet down and return to normal. You can still live a good life in this beautiful place."

"But I don't *want* to stay!" Te' cried. She turned to face Manaia and scowled. "I will *never* love that man. You're the only one that I want."

"Oh Te'—" I said, trying to hold back my tears.

Te's father suddenly motioned to the guards, and they grabbed her arms, pulling her away from me. I despaired at the thought of never speaking with her again and reached into my handbag, passing her my card.

"I don't know if you can send mail via the cargo ship, but this has my address if you want to keep in touch."

The boatmen started up the engine and pushed the skiff off the beach, and my face tightened in anguish as Teuila screamed and flailed, trying to escape the guards' grasp. I blew her a kiss and mouthed the words I love you, then the boat turned around and headed toward the cargo ship over the bumpy surf. When we reached the big ship, they threw a rope ladder over the side and I leaned over the gunwales, retching into the sea. I couldn't bear the thought of never seeing my island girl again.

After I got on deck, I peered over the railing toward the village lagoon, but Teuila was nowhere to be seen. For a brief moment, I considered asking the crew to drop me off on the other side of the island, then I realized I'd just be prolonging her agony. I asked the porter to escort me to my stateroom, where I cried myself to sleep.

33

It took me four full days to return home to Chicago. I had to have new credit cards delivered to a branch of my bank in Honiara, then take three flights to transport me from the Solomon Islands back to the continental USA via Sydney and Hawaii. But I was in no hurry to return to the comforts of my previous life. I didn't even buy new clothes en route to the States, happy to wear my tapa dress for a few more days as my fellow fliers looked on curiously.

It wasn't until I'd been home for a few weeks that I began to settle in to my normal routine. But I never stopped thinking of Teuila. Whenever I passed the pineapple stand in my local grocery store, I smiled recalling how she'd scaled the prickly tree to harvest some fruit for us to eat near our favorite waterhole. I cooked seafood on my barbeque and marinated it in lime juice, trying to remember how good the fresh-caught grouper tasted after we'd trapped it in the lagoon. But the only tangible memento I had of her was my little unicorn shell, which I placed on my office desk and gently caressed whenever I needed to let my mind wander back to the pristine waters of our private paradise.

One particularly lonely day, I opened the photo app on my iPhone, intending to browse through the few pictures I'd taken of Anuta before getting lost in the jungle. I knew that I didn't have any photos of Teuila, but I wanted to see the pink sand and big leafy trees of the island again to remind me of the few blissful days we'd shared in our lagoon. I smiled at the pictures of Captain Ben and the rest of the crew of our sailing vessel, and my heart skipped a beat looking at the images of my fellow passengers enjoying our first catch in the lagoon.

But as I flipped through the pictures, my eyes suddenly widened when I came upon some photos of Manaia hunched over one of the village's dugout canoes as smoke poured from the inner hull. I paused for a moment, dumbfounded at how the villagers had figured out how to use the sophisticated electronic device. I knew that young children could quickly decipher the graphical user interface, and I assumed that one of Te's siblings had picked up my unlocked phone and begun playing with it before it ran out of battery power. The camera app was at the top of the screen, and they must have accidentally tapped the capture button while running around the courtyard.

I studied the photos for a moment and spread my fingers to zoom in on the images. The pictures provided unmistakable proof that Manaia had sabotaged the canoes shortly before the battle with the other tribe. But what could I do with them? I could try printing the images and sending them back to Teuila and her father. But how would that change anything? He'd just think it was another trick by the jealous American, who was manipulating her Western technology to accuse a rival of violating their custom of Aropa.

But I couldn't just stand by and do nothing. If there was the slightest chance to use the pictures to convict Manaia of his crimes, maybe the chief would excommunicate him from the tribe, or at least annul his marriage to his daughter. And if the wedding was overturned, this could open a window for me to return to the island and reclaim my girl. I rushed to the nearest photo shop and asked to have the pictures developed immediately then called the shipping company that had picked me up from Anuta to see when the next ship would be passing by the island. They said another ship was scheduled to return the following month and that they could deliver a package to the island for a fee.

I mailed them the photos together with a bank draft for two hundred dollars, with explicit instructions to deliver the package to the chief's daughter only. Concerned they might just take my money and run, I told them if they could return a note from Teuila, I'd send them another two hundred dollars as proof of delivery. Four hundred bucks was a pretty steep price to send a package overseas, but it would be worth it for my peace of mind knowing that her father at least had tangible proof of Manaia's treachery.

I waited over a month for some kind of word back from Teuila. Then another month passed. And another. Eventually, I resigned myself to the fact that there was nothing further I could do to convince the chief of Manaia's lack of fitness for his daughter. For weeks, I cried myself to sleep every night pining for my lost love, realizing that I'd never see her again. It seemed ironic that *I* was the one having difficulty letting go, not her.

Then one day, returning from running some errands, I noticed a shiny stone lying atop the welcome mat in front of my front door. I squinted at the object, then widened my eyes, recognizing the familiar shape. I picked up the gem and ran my fingers around the edges as my heart began to thump in my chest. It looked just like the stone Te' had picked up off the beach of our lagoon and said she'd keep it as a memento of our love.

I suddenly gasped and swung around to see Teuila's pretty face smiling at me.

Ready for more lesbian romance and erotica? Check out the entire collection of stories in Jade's Erotic Adventures in your favorite online bookstore: